COOL

# COOLIE

## 'If Allah has ordained it thus...?'

BY

MADELON H. LULOFS

*Author of 'Rubber'*

TRANSLATED FROM THE DUTCH BY

G. J. RENIER AND

IRENE CLEPHANE

WITH A FOREWORD BY

ANTHONY REID

SINGAPORE

OXFORD UNIVERSITY PRESS

OXFORD NEW YORK

*Oxford University Press, Walton Street, Oxford* OX2 6DP

*Oxford New York Toronto*
*Delhi Bombay Calcutta Madras Karachi*
*Kuala Lumpur Singapore Hong Kong Tokyo*
*Nairobi Dar es Salaam Cape Town*
*Melbourne Auckland Madrid*

*and associated companies in*
*Berlin Ibadan*

*Oxford is a trade mark of Oxford University Press*



*Originally published in Holland as 'Koelie'*
*English translation first published in 1936*
*by Cassell & Co. Ltd.*

*Reissued as an Oxford University Press paperback 1982*
*Sixth impression 1993*

*ISBN 0 19 582528 4*



*Printed in Malaysia by Peter Chong Printers Sdn. Bhd.*
*Published by Oxford University Press Pte. Ltd.,*
*Unit 221, Ubi Avenue 4, Singapore 1440*

# FOREWORD

MADELON HERMINA LULOFS (1899–1958) was born in Surabaya and spent almost all of the first thirty years of her life in Indonesia. Holland, as she wrote later, was then only the place for 'home' leave. Her father, the prominent Netherlands Indies official C. Lulofs, took her from post to post—sometimes in remote districts where they were the only European family, sometimes in the big colonial cities. At the age of nineteen she was thrown into the isolated life of a rubber planter's wife on the southern fringes of the 'plantation district' of East Sumatra. During her time (1918–1930) amidst the rubber plantations of Asahan, about 125 km south of Medan, this was still a harsh frontier region, even though the longer-developed tobacco area around Medan was beginning to take on a more settled and relaxed character.

In 1930 she scandalized the colonial society of East Sumatra by leaving her planter husband for a then-unknown Hungarian, László Székely. As a sensitive 'outsider' in East Sumatra during its pioneering days, Székely had written a fine novel, *Tropic Fever* (reprinted, OUP, Kuala Lumpur, 1979), though few were aware of it since the book had not yet been translated out of its original Hungarian.

Only after settling in Europe with her new husband did Mrs Székely-Lulofs (as she became known in Holland) begin to write about the society she had left. Within three years she had produced four books—*Rubber* in 1931, *Koelie* (*Coolie*) in 1932, *Emigranten* (*Emigrants*) and *De Andere Wereld* (*The Other World*) in 1933. The first two caused a great sensation, partly because they seemed immediately relevant to the 'colonial question' in general and to the controversial 'penal sanction' for labour contracts in East Sumatra in particular. *Rubber* was published in several languages and made into a Dutch play and film, despite being denounced as distortion by the 'Sumatra lobby' in Holland. *Coolie* evoked similar responses, as is clear from the author's preface.

*Rubber*, like Székely's *Tropic Fever*, carries authority because it is semi-autobiographical, dealing from the inside with the often unlovely lives of the Europeans on the estates. *Coolie* attempts the much more difficult task of trying to enter the mental world of the captive labourers from Java, whose passivity and resignation, punctuated by outbursts of desperate violence, was extremely difficult for their European overlords to understand. Of course it fails, sometimes falling into the planter stereotypes of which the author is elsewhere scornful. Her later historical novel about the Achinese guerrilla heroine Tjut Nja Din (1948), about whom she had no first-hand knowledge, is a more impressive feat of careful scholarship and imagination. It received the compliment of a post-independence Indonesian translation by Abdul Moeis (1954).

Nevertheless *Coolie* springs direct and fresh from a wealth of experience on the estates. We need have no doubt that all of the incidents described were real ones, nor that the attempt to give them meaning in the life of 'Ruki' was honest and well intentioned. The labourers of Sumatra left no memoirs of their own. Whatever the limitations of this book, we have no better material for attempting to visualise the extraordinarily harsh world of the Sumatran estate labour force in the early decades of this century.

*Australian National University* ANTHONY REID
*Canberra*
*May 1981*

## A WORD TO MY BRITISH READERS

IN Holland and in the Dutch Colonies my novel *Coolie* has been misunderstood by some people. They concluded that it was my intention to criticize a particular aspect of Dutch colonial policy, namely, the recruiting of contract coolies in the Island of Java for work on the plantations of Sumatra. In order to avoid a similar misunderstanding abroad, I wish to say that *Coolie* is not a political novel. Its intention is purely literary.

I have tried to fathom and to express the various shapes adopted by the human soul as a result of different circumstances. In other words, I have studied the way in which the soul reacts to destiny. A human being is to me a human being, whether white, brown, red, yellow, or black. To understand the level of culture and civilization he has reached, and the place to which he is entitled in consequence, are two entirely different problems. For me the human soul remains the main thing. The finest task before the writer of a book is that of examining and formulating the problems of the human soul.

Such was my conscious intention in writing *Coolie*. The theme is not the subjection of coloured races to the white man. It is not an indictment of the

West or a defence of the East. It is an attempt to explain the soul of a strange race that still remains mysterious to us of the West. I had no political aims in view. I merely observed the disturbance caused in the mind of the Oriental confronted with the Western régime—victim of a more or less necessary system. Moreover, the contract system and the penal sanctions by which it was supported were abolished by the Dutch Government in 1931.

May the unprejudiced reader realize my point of view, and may the reading of this book contribute to clarifying a psychology that is still almost unknown to us!

MADELON H. LULOFS

# PART I

# I

BEHIND the pasture-land rose the volcano, blue against the blue sky. But it was a different blue. It was a soft pastel tint compared to the fierce primitive colour of the sky. Despite its blueness, the tall cone seemed to have grown out of the green undulations of the grassland. It was as though once upon a time earth had miraculously lost its motionless rigidity and had suddenly lifted heavenward one single column of its own whirling material. It was as though one desire, striving high, had been solidified into a perpetual monument of the quest after the ideal.

Since that time, the volcano had risen slender and graceful from the plain which it seemed to guard and to contemplate, and to keep safe from the world. The grassland had become a world in itself: an untamed world of coarse, harsh grass and ragged bushes on which grew tiny orange-yellow flowers. The little Sundanese boys had a rude name for them: they called them tai-ajam—chicken droppings—because, they said, the stench of the flowers was described by the name.

Mimosa rioted underneath and all over the bushes, spreading everywhere its long thorny branches, its fine rosy down, and the tender dark green leaflets which shrank together, with a prudish and over-sensitive gesture, at the slightest touch.

There were ditches and hollows at unexpected places, and tiny hillocks that made one wonder why they had appeared precisely where they were. There they stood, in the centre of a completely level plain, pretentious, and a little ridiculous by the side of the divine majesty of the miraculously created volcano. These hillocks had risen through the tireless industry of myriads of ants, and had immediately been over-grown by the harsh grass and the relentless mimosa. Here and there also were pools where the buffaloes bathed and sheltered from the burning sun. The animals plunged their ungainly grey bodies into the greasy black slush which was barely covered by the green slimy water that crawled with mosquito larvæ and leeches. They were sucked down by the gurgling mud until only their heads with their large cruel horns emerged.

In one place, an old, neglected native cemetery displayed its small oblong mounds, most of them pathetic, puny child-graves. Along the sides of the graves white pebbles were arranged, at the heads stood weathered boards. On some lay the skeleton of a pajong, a paper parasol once placed on the ground as a humble token of respect for death, and now almost dissolved by the rains. Among the tai-ajam bushes which had shot up among the graves stood a churchyard-tree, meagre, twisted, with a thin trunk and dark shiny leaves. From its branches sprang a few pale yellow, magnolia-like flowers, dying like the little dying cemetery.

Some way farther on was a bamboo hedge. There, from the impoverished soil, rose a small group of banana trees, too degenerate to bear fruit. In days gone by there had been a campong on this spot, but the inhabitants had moved on when the soil grew too exhausted to germinate their seed. They had left everything as they had known it. The rain had fallen, the houses had rotted away and disappeared, strong growing weeds had stifled the cultivated plants of the little gardens. Nothing remained except that bit of hedge, these fruit trees, and the cemetery—sad relics of human habitation—themselves awaiting inevitable dissolution. Slowly the landscape was slipping back into the all-embracing womb of the earth, the strong, the untamed mother of things born of the gods.

Through a deep ravine between the volcano and the plain meandered the river, hidden by graceful, waving bamboo canes, and above everything was the sky, quivering in the glow of the sun.

Over the grassland the buffaloes roamed in herds, heavy, prehistoric-looking beasts moving their lazy, sombre, mud-stained bodies at a slow pace and lifting their powerful horned heads only to stare greedily at the distant blue of the volcano or at the wide plain that glowed and trembled in the singeing glare of the sun.

Among the Sundanese boys who guarded the buffaloes was Ruki. Like the others, he sat on the broad back of a beast and his dark, earnest, mysterious eyes gazed dreamily into the hot sunny day.

His slender, pale brown body was almost naked. He wore nothing but a pair of torn, ragged shorts, kept in place round his waist by a twisted rope of bark, tied below his prominent rice-filled belly. His rough black hair grew abundantly on his pointed head and hung down in wisps over his face.

Half asleep, half awake, he sat chewing a grass stem as he was carried by the slow, cradling motion of the buffalo, whose body, on which the mud had dried in colourless lumps and streaks, was deliciously warm. His own body was deliciously warm too, caressed by the broiling heat. The pores of his skin stood wide open, and the sweat poured in rivulets down his bare back. Ruki delighted in this blessing of life which made his body supple and healthy. "Those who cannot have a good sweat carry a dull and unwilling body about with them," said Ruki's nenneh, his old grandmother.

Ruki's mother had died at his birth, and his father had naturally taken another wife immediately. Ruki's father's new wife was young and healthy. She bore children at once, and Ruki therefore was no longer needed. That is why he lived with his nenneh, who was old. Later, when nenneh became very old and he was a man, he would be able to look after her. For is it not with this aim in view that Allah continually creates new generations lest the aged should go hungry and uncared for?

But such thoughts were not in Ruki's head. There really were no thoughts in his head. He was sitting on the back of his buffalo chewing a grass stem and dangling his thin arms and legs limply. The day was good. The sun was good. His belly was bulging with the rice nenneh had cooked for him. Fair was the grassland, the sky, the mountain, the bamboo by the river, the campong in the valley. And behind the campong lay several small rice-fields. Bees hummed among the flowers of the tai-ajam; the buffaloes grazed over the wide plain, scarcely moving at all. Such was Ruki's whole world, and it was a good world.

A bird settled on a buffalo's broad head and pecked at the ticks between the animal's horns. Ruki did not chase it away. The buffalo continued to graze unconcernedly. Mosquitoes danced before Ruki's eyes. A leech was sucking blood from the calf of his leg: he did not notice. Over him was the rigid vast sky. In it hung the sun, a glowing yellow disk. All was still. No sound, no breeze slipped through the trembling heat. Everything lay broiling and basking in the sun. Everything was good because Allah had ordained it thus.

The day was long. How many hours . . . .? This Ruki could not have said. It was day from sunrise to sunset. When the blue of the sky above the volcano grew red, the evening was near. When the light stole away from the plain, when the bees suddenly disappeared and the buffaloes lifted their heads and uttered a brief, raucous bellow . . . when the evil spirits wrapped themselves in their misty cloaks and began to roam over the land, then Ruki and his young companions knew that it was time to go home, to bathe, to say a prayer, to eat, and to sleep. For the night, the dark, moonless night, was not made by Allah for mankind.

Then Ruki slipped off the back of his buffalo. The animal joined the herd, which stayed out in the grassland, and together with the other boys he returned to the campong.

At one spot the grassland narrowed to a gully. Here a steep narrow footpath plunged into the dark depths where the bamboo grew. In this damp cool shade stood the campong, and at the roots of the bamboo canes the river rushed over colossal boulders and lumps of rock thrown out by the volcano in one of its eruptions.

Ruki and his companions pulled off their dirty shorts and jumped into the stream. Only now did their minds awaken. Every night they became once more playful, alert, and bold as children, abandoning for the moment the full, ripe, philosophic, mystical spirit that belongs to the East. They jumped from stone to stone, clambered rocks with springing feet, splashed the water and threw it at one another. Their young, shrill voices rose louder than the voice of the river. Their shining brown bodies became one with the brown water and the brown banks and the shadows created by evening. They pursued each other over the sandbank and, bursting with laughter, they floundered in the deep gully where their feet did not touch the ground. Their exuberant joy melted into the monotonous prayer of their elders who stood, their closed hands pressed against their faces, turned towards Mecca, until they sank down to the earth, kissing it again and again with the devotion of the orthodox, god-fearing, natural man.

When tiny red oil lamps began to shine in the small dark houses, the boys dressed. Some wrapped themselves in sarongs with batik designs; the poorer ones merely put on their shorts again. As they left the water, they shook off all childishness. Quiet and self-possessed, almost dignified, they squatted down in the circle of men who had gathered in the small public place of the campong and, like them, they rolled their cigarettes, using a maize leaf instead of paper. While they smoked they talked of all the important things in their small world. Their voices were deep and never noisy, but there was no melancholy in them. They were people of the fertile Java mountains. Each of them owned his morsel of land across the river. Each of them had a buffalo and a little house of bamboo and leaves.

Their chief care was the cutting of the paddy; their chief sorrow the loss of a buffalo dragged away by a tiger. For without a buffalo no ploughing could be done. When a child was born, they made a feast, a slamatan. And also when somebody died. For Allah gives and Allah takes away. Their laughter was rare, their tears were rarer. Their earnestness was that of an animal which passes its days contented and without desire, trustful of life and happy therefore without awareness of happiness. Their contentment found utterance in one way only: in the sound of their speech, which is light and melodious like the latent song of the pure mountain wind and the sweet warmth of the sun.

The small public square was dry and dusty. Two rainless months had dried the clay of the soil and pitted it with bizarrely shaped cracks. The campong houses stood round about higgledy-piggledy. On eight bamboo stakes stood a platform of rough boards, to which led rickety steps. The walls of the little houses were of bamboo, split and plaited, the roof was of palm leaves. Three great heaps of refuse stood among the houses. Fruit trees shot up from them, grown out of stones that had been thrown away and had germinated lustily in the hot manure. There was a well surrounded by a tottering railing. From this the campong dwellers drew their drinking water. There also, when the river, swollen by the rains, rushed past dangerously, the women washed their clothes. By the side of each house was a smouldering bonfire of grass and leaves, and the acrid smoke rose up towards the dwellings and crept in through every cranny of the floors and of the walls. It also spread across the little square and drove away some of the mosquitoes that came in swarms from the dark bamboo plantation.

Somewhere behind one of the houses a man was singing. Dreamy, pious sounds dripped into the evening: it was a melody of primitive fatalism cast in a minor key. Cicadas shrilled their ear-splitting song. A goat was bleating. Hens and chickens clucked and cackled as they sought roosting places on the roofs or on the laths under the houses. A pregnant cat dragged its heavy belly over the ground and disappeared into a dark corner. Emaciated dogs with great wounds and mangy spots sniffed in the gutters and among the refuse and nosed into the few empty tins that lay scattered about. A rat scurried along the top of a door. A child that was being bathed howled with the full force of its lungs. It was loudly scolded by its mother, who held it in one arm while with the other hand she dipped water with an old paraffin tin and poured it over the child. The stench of rancid coconut oil, dried fish, and manure rotting back to soil beat through the atmosphere, which grew moister and moister.

And suddenly night fell.

Above the men's heads, at the top of one of the flights of steps, appeared an old woman bent nearly double.

"Now then, come along home!" she grumbled. "It's quite dark. Must you stay out again till the vapours rise from the river and make you ill? And you've still got to open the coconut for me."

Ruki glanced over his shoulder. He made no reply. Quietly he finished the native cigarette he was smoking. He had long been aware of his manhood, and of that sense of male superiority which never take women quite seriously. He yawned, stretched, and one by one cracked his fingers in all their joints. Then he scratched his head. He scratched his head with both hands, slowly, voluptuously, all over the skull. Then he rose, pulled up his shorts, which threatened to slip down over his narrow hips, and tied them more securely round his loins.

Without a word he left the circle and climbed the steps. A moment later he appeared again with a coconut and a parang—a sharp hatchet. With a few skilful blows he beheaded the coconut, poured away the liquid, and split the fruit in two.

Nenneh was busy in her little kitchen. It stood on the ground with the walls reaching only half-way up to the slanting roof, which rested on bamboo stakes. It contained an oven built of bricks, and on a flaming wood fire stood the tall copper rice-boiler. She was bending over a black iron pan in which she was frying some small dried fish. The ruddy glow of the fire played over her and transformed her into a witch. The feeble light of the smoky lamp suspended from a rusty nail was swallowed up by the glow. Myriads of insects swarmed around her. Through the hiss of the frying oil sounded the loud clucking of a hen as she settled down in a dirty old basket with her chicks under her warm maternal body.

Ruki helped to grate the coconut. Nenneh put the grated flesh into a bowl, poured water on it, kneaded it and pressed it through a sieve. The milky substance thus produced was used to prepare a vegetable sauce that went with the rice.

A little later Ruki took his meal squatting down on the floor. His nimble fingers kneaded a bit of rice into a little ball and carried it to his mouth. With his fingers also he divided the fish; while the vegetable sauce he sipped from a little cup. Then he washed his hands in a finger-bowl, rinsed his mouth, and rolled himself a native cigarette, using a maize leaf as wrapping. He took up an easier attitude, crossing his legs on the floor that was covered by a mat. The little oil wick was burning by his side, spreading a narrow circle of light around him. The rest of the room lay steeped in darkness. The atmosphere was heavy with smoke, and with the odours of cooked food, and of the sharp, sweet native tobacco. The narrow wooden shutter and the door had been carefully closed in order to guard against harmful vapours and evil spirits. Mosquitoes buzzed in their hundreds.

Ruki sat staring at the light with wide, unseeing eyes. Now and then he carefully squashed a mosquito that had settled on his hand or his face. He belched loudly several times, for he had had a good meal.

"Come and sleep," said nenneh, "it is late. There is no use in being awake when it is dark. In seven days there will be full moon, and then you can stay awake."

Ruki rose. He took an old sarong, wrapped it round his well-made, fourteen-year-old body, and laid himself down by nenneh's side on the wooden sleeping couch. Under them was a mat, and their heads lay on little pillows that were greasy and smelt of coconut oil. Beneath nenneh's pillow was a dirty, green silk handkerchief. In one of its corners was knotted some small change. Under the pillow also were a batik sarong and a black cotton jacket. This, and an old tin in which nenneh kept tobacco and betel nut, formed their only property, together with the house, the buffalo, the rice-field, the hen and her chicks. And it was all they needed.

Everything that Ruki knew he had learned from nenneh. She had also explained to him how Allah has arranged the relationship between man and woman. It is all very simple and natural. There is nothing shameful in it because all things Allah has created are good and simple and natural, and surely it is for the purpose of instructing the young that the old have been made.

But before Ruki fell asleep a slow thought passed through his head. It was the first thought of the day.

He had learned something which nenneh had not taught him. This morning he had seen Supinah bathing in the river. She was still young, as young as he. She was still a child. Her sarong had been all wet, and had clung to her slender body. He had noticed the incipient beauty thus betrayed. He had seen her long blue-black hair as she undid it from the knot, and suddenly he had known the thing nenneh could never have taught him: desire for the young, untouched body of a girl.

## II

THE paddy was ripening.

The stalks were still green, but the heavy ears were already bending towards the ground. Ruki had built himself a little tent. It was a platform of plaited bamboo high upon stakes with a roof made out of an old clout. He lay there stretched out on his back. From a rice stalk he had made himself a little flute. It gave only one note—tu-tu—but that was enough for Ruki. He blew uninterruptedly, tu-tu, and the shrill sound flew away into the wide quiet day.

From the little tent, a skilful net of fine white threads ran right across the whole rice-field. Many-coloured rags were tied to the threads, and whenever a troop of chattering, winged thieves prepared to settle on the rice, Ruki moved the threads hither and thither so that the rags waved and frightened away the little birds. It was easy work. All the threads were attached to one string tied round his big toe. Otherwise he would have had to hold the ends of the threads in his hands, which would have meant sitting up all day. Why sit up if the work can be done equally well lying down? It is far better to lie down and to pipe tu-tu-tu throughout the day.

Besides, he could look up at the sky. There were glare clouds drifting slowly past far above their shadows that moved across the landscape. Sometimes a reddish hawk circled high up in the air. Its head inclined downwards, it sought its prey. Ruki watched with concentration for the moment when the bird was about to drop, and he waited till it shot down like an arrow from a bow. Then he screamed, "Ou-ie, ou-ie!"

At once the ulung-ulung interrupted its fall like a perfect acrobat who commands every muscle of his body. Then it wheeled in a wide arc and flew up again, taking refuge in the infinite blue.

Each time this happened Ruki grinned with satisfaction. Hidden deep in his primitive, kindly nature there was the first seed of something belonging to a higher culture: the desire to tease. He did not act out of pity for the prey that was torn to pieces by the sharp talons of the ulung-ulung. He only knew the joy of thwarting the bird of prey. It was an unconscious exercise of the sense of power.

The sun stewed the paddy into ripeness. A warm vapour shimmered between heaven and earth.

The volcano was blue, blue. . . .

These things Ruki did not see. Why should he notice them? Ever since he had come into the world, there had been this mountain with its tall, blue cone round which hung an occasional feather of diaphanous smoke. It never did any harm. His whole world had always been blue and green, and, when the paddy was ripening, yellow. These were the holy colours of fertility. Two only of them had any meaning in his eyes: green stood for young paddy, yellow for the approaching harvest.

It was lovely to lie down there without thoughts, simply to be! To be, throughout the whole sunny day. Late in the afternoon he had to cut grass for the buffalo. He knew the time of day by the clouds that gathered round the crater of the volcano. Nenneh had made him build a little stable for the buffalo where it spent the night. A neighbour's beast had been carried away, and nenneh would no longer allow hers to stay out in the open during the night. This was the only difference there had been in Ruki's life for the last three years. He was a real man now. Seventeen years old—if nenneh was right in reckoning the moons that had been full since his birth. Soon he would be married, to Supinah. When the paddy had been cut.

It was full moon that night.

The little square of the campong was unusually animated. The men were smoking and their talk was louder than usual. A dog howled. Restless shadows wandered among the silhouettes of the houses. The bamboo showed like some exquisite lace against the moonlit dome of the sky.

As Ruki came walking towards the campong with a bundle of grass on his shoulder, he felt surprised. He did not hear the gamelan. It was full moon, and there was no gamelan! Was there no prayer either?

He hastened his step, involuntarily. He hurried for the first time in his life. And as he passed the circle of men he noticed at once that there was a stranger among them. He stopped out of curiosity. The newcomer was from Batavia. Ruki heard him say so. He spoke with a foreign accent. But how well dressed he was, thought Ruki. . . . He wore a rustling, brightly-coloured sarong. Also a starched white coat such as only the tuan Controller wore. And moreover he had a red velvet cap, and no turban.

Ruki was surprised, and felt a sense of shame. No turban! But that was against the custom. When a man wears such fine clothes, he should wear a turban.

Ruki hurried with the grass to the stable, and spread it out for the buffalo. He returned to the square at once without bathing, and squatted down among the others, who were listening with rapt attention to the stranger.

"And then there are fire wagons of iron, and houses made of stone."

"Ts . . . ts . . . ts!" said the campong dwellers, full of amazement. They forgot to puff at their cigarettes, which went out in their hands.

"Those who come to that new land, to Deli, can buy much gold. Gold is cheap there. And there are many young and lovely women. And then one is allowed to gamble there."

"Waah!" The cry of delighted surprise came as from one mouth. Every one of these men and boys had gambling in his blood. They were all born dice throwers. But the Government had forbidden gambling in Java.

"But won't the police take you away if you play with dice?" asked one old man wonderingly.

"Indeed no," replied the stranger. "Allah is my

witness when I say that you may play with dice there. Just as much as you like."

"Waah!" They trembled with feverish ecstasy.

"All those who have gone have come back wealthy a few years later."

The men were silent.

The moon shone upon their tense faces with the childlike, astonished eyes. But something new had appeared in those eyes: they told of covetousness.

Had covetousness sprung up so quickly? Dice! Gold! Young women! How could it be otherwise? Covetousness scarcely born was already at work in their slow minds, which were puzzled by the new thought gripping their heads and their hearts: the thought of possession.

"What is life in a campong like this?" asked the stranger, disparagingly. "What do you men know of life? Or of the world? You . . . why, you know only your river and your house. You eat nothing but your plate of rice and a morsel of fish. You wear ungainly clothes. Now just take a look at me. What are you but poor miserable creatures? How much land do you own? What . . .? Do your women wear gold coins? Have your children gold and silver bangles round their ankles? Tell me, when it is slamatan among you, how many goats do you kill? Not more than one, eh?"

Ashamed, the men bent their heads in silence. The stranger poured out the venom drop by drop, poisoning the peace and contentment of their dreamy existence.

"And women? Maidens? Has not each of you older men a wife as old as himself?"

Their hazy thoughts grew restless. An unwonted fieriness crept into their gestures, usually so reserved. Their voices rose. They forgot the evening meal. They talked loudly, all together. They laughed with excitement and repeated the stranger's words.

"Maidens!"

The women and the girls moved stealthily nearer. What was this stranger talking about that made their husbands and brothers behave so oddly?

Nenneh stood there too, bent and trembling. In the sharp blue moonlight she looked like an old witch. Her scraggy neck sprang forward from her stooping shoulders. Her head was nearly bald, her mouth was toothless. In her cheek bulged a wad of betel, and her lips were carmined with its juice. Her black jacket was open, displaying her shrunken, wrinkled, hanging breasts. Two fiery eyes looked out of her ravaged face: they were observing the man from Batavia with suspicion and disapproval. Then, to show her contempt, she spat out a broad blood-red jet of betel, and, clenching her bony hand into a fist, she suddenly shouted to the men: "Don't you allow that lying dog to drive you crazy with his talk. It's easy to tell pretty tales. Yes, but what are you doing here? Leave our men alone. Young women, virgins, they need not go away to look for them. We've enough of them in our own campong."

A murmur of approval came from the women and the girls. They sensed an unknown danger.

"Old wives' talk!" exclaimed the stranger contemptuously.

Ruki looked up. He was ashamed of his grandmother. "Go home and cook," he said to her roughly.

"Cook!" shouted nenneh excitedly. "Cook, eh? Hasn't the food been ready this long while, you son of a pig? Perhaps the fish is not growing tough and uneatable? Perhaps the sauce has not been made? But you can't come home in good time. You must listen to the idle chatter of this nasty town crocodile, that's what you must do. Along with you! Get home!" She pulled Ruki by his jacket. With a quick movement, he wrenched himself loose.

"Leave me alone," he said, imperiously but quietly. "Go back to your kitchen and don't meddle with what is the business of men."

Nenneh retreated muttering and scolding. Her old spindle legs tottered under her as she climbed the steps. As she reached the top, she turned round and spat again, and after this gesture of supreme contempt she disappeared into the house.

The stranger had a good look at Ruki.

"You're a bold young man!" he said approvingly, placing his jewelled hand for a moment on Ruki's shoulder.

Ruki's heart swelled with pride. He noticed the envious looks of the others, and he expanded his chest. He threw back his head, and, placing a hand on his hip, he bragged: "I'm not afraid of anybody or anything." He felt that the men of his campong were proud because they could show the stranger that they had such a bold young man among them.

The man from Batavia called again on the following night, and on the night after that. They fed him generously. They listened to his exciting stories of the wonderful land far away of which they dreamed during their restless sleep.

Ruki was lying with his hands beneath his head. He stared into the darkness in which the little smoky wick floating in oil traced a very small circle of light. The mosquitoes were singing round his ears their high-pitched song of desire and greed. Outside a cicada was chirping in the bamboo canes. He could not sleep. His little pillow, though he turned it round again and again, glowed under his cheek. His breath was heavy in the heavy atmosphere. He was not really thinking, he merely ruminated words: "Wealth. Women. Cheap gold. Dice." Wherever his eyes turned in the darkness he saw images. He did not consider what he should do with his wealth. The women did not appear before him as something clearly defined. He felt only a longing that made him restless. Maybe there was an unconscious thirst for adventure. He had never seen anything outside the campong. He tried to picture what existed beyond; but he could not. He could not see, therefore he did not know. He had never needed to think. What was there for him to think about? All he needed he had—the house, the couch, the plate of rice, the warm sun, the fertilizing rain, the carefree day, the long night made for sleep.

He tossed restlessly. Nenneh muttered in her sleep as he touched her by accident.

He listened to the mosquitoes, to a rat gnawing a hole somewhere. He listened to the woodworms working ceaselessly in one of the feet of the couch. Then suddenly he thought he heard a gentle knock. He raised his head. His concentrated attention pierced the darkness. The knock was repeated, gentle but definite. He heard it, perhaps, more with his soul, which was suddenly wide awake for the first time, than with his ears. For the first time his soul was roused from its indolence.

Ruki rose, stole past nenneh with the utmost care, and softly opened the door. Under the steps stood the stranger. Behind him were two boys from the village, Sidin and Karimun.

"We're off now," the stranger whispered; "are you coming too?"

Ruki hesitated. He looked round at the little room where nenneh lay asleep. It was an unconscious gesture, an attempt to find help from familiar things.

"We are going," said Karimun. There was the pride of a man in his voice.

"I'm coming with you," answered Ruki. "Wait just one moment." He went into the house again. From beneath nenneh's little pillow he carefully pulled out the new sarong and put it on. From a shelf he took a piece of cake, wrapped it in a banana leaf, and slipped it into his pocket. Then, without looking back, he slipped out of the house and closed the door soundlessly.

The four men marched silently one behind the other. It was nearly morning, but the moon was still bright. Its harsh white light poured along the narrow leaves of the coconut palms, slipped down from the roofs of the dark houses, and made the little square into one large blob of white. Plunged in this pool of still, silvery light, the campong slept heavily. Motionless before the hour of awakening, everything dreamed its last devout dream. The frail brown houses stood on their tottering stakes beneath their knotted roofs. The banana plantation received the beams of the moon upon the shields of its broad, smooth leaves. The coconut palms raised their tall stems into the air and burst suddenly into leaf as though they were rockets. The bamboo canes were a delicate fretwork of thin, sharp leaves. The river rushed by, stroking the great boulders in its bed. The pale disk of the moon, slightly flattened on one side, stood out against the transparent blue sky. In the serene silence, a cicada chirped on a drowsy note.

Then the first soft morning breeze swept over the still world, rustled through the bamboo canes, caressed the coconut palms, the banana trees, the roofs of the houses. A leaf of a coconut palm woke up and began to tremble violently. A cock crowed, and suddenly a dog began to bark furiously. Ruki kicked it. The animal slunk away with a howl and took refuge beneath a house.

They followed the narrow path that led to the grasslands. A drab light, made up of the disappearing silver and the approaching red, hung over the land. A bank of cloud enveloped the volcano. Above the cloud lay the crater, a tenuous line against the colourless sky. From the plain that seemed endless rose a damp mist, and very far away vague outlines emerged from it. They were buffaloes. A chill wind made the men shiver. Ruki unfastened his sarong and drew it high over his shoulders. Mixed with the discomfort caused by the cold, he felt a vague melancholy. For a moment he thought of his buffalo. Who would cut the grass for it to-night?

Just then the man from Batavia offered him a cigarette. Ruki grinned. So far he had never smoked anything except native cigarettes wrapped in maize leaves which he rolled for himself. Awkwardly he turned the machine-made cigarette round in his fingers, casting a sidelong glance at Sidin and Karimun. These two had already put theirs in their mouths and were blowing out the smoke through their nostrils. Ruki asked them for a light, and a moment later he was smoking too.

"How do you like it?" asked the stranger, glancing back over his shoulder, for they were still marching in single file.

"It's good," said Ruki, hiding the giddiness caused by the tobacco, so different from that to which he was accustomed.

"Just wait till you get outside this hole of a place. Then you'll see some sights worth seeing. You'll eat meat and chicken. You'll wear silken sarongs. You'll have three lovely young women. Why, you'll have four! You just mark my words."

The man from Batavia leaned to one side and spat

as an indication of his contempt for the wretched life his companions had hitherto led.

Through the uncertain morning light, the day suddenly broke. The sun appeared blood red above the horizon. The mist flowed away and dissolved. The grass lay bathed in dew. The moon melted into the radiant sky as the sun climbed up in triumph. The volcano showed violet against the red-gold light. Then, as the red-gold slowly faded, it turned to blue against the blue sky. An hour later the whole landscape was broiling in the sun.

The four men walked past the rice-fields. There was no path—only the embankment along the fields. The heat that rose up to them from the tall, nearly ripe paddy seemed to come from a hot-house. Tiny campongs nestled among the rice-fields in the shade of the banyan trees.

Ruki and his friends were already outside the land they knew. But in the background still stood the volcano, which seemed to walk along with them, a guide on their expedition, a protection but also a warning. Now and then Ruki glanced round. Without being aware of it, he was glad to see the mountain there: it lulled a vague sense of discomfort which he was loth to display.

Suddenly the stranger stepped down from the embankment and took a narrow meandering footpath that went through hedges and undergrowth till it met the government road, a broad thoroughfare of shiny white flints. Carts with squeaking axles passed slowly along it, swaying and screeching on their wheels. On the bottom of each cart, under a little roof of leaves, sat its driver. Most of them were asleep, wrapped to the chin in their sarongs. The rope with which they guided ox or buffalo hung slack in their hands. Several Sundanese walked by, balancing over their shoulders bamboo rods weighed down at each end by heavy baskets full of fruit and vegetables.

"They're going to market," said the man from Batavia, pointing to them. "In a few hours we shall reach the first small town. There we shall get into the fire wagon."

"I'm hungry," said Karimun diffidently.

"We'll have some food in a moment," the stranger assured him. By the side of the road stood a little shop, a mere stall made of bamboo canes and leaves, where an old woman was selling food. She had set it out on a wobbly table, and in front of the table stood a rough wooden bench. "Sit down and choose just what you like. I'm paying."

Ruki and his friends helped themselves greedily to the unfamiliar delicacies. They had never before eaten so much or such good food. It cheered them up and made them feel gay. The man from Batavia paid. With an indifferent gesture he took a handful of silver—guilders and rix-dollars—from his pocket. Karimun nudged his companions. Eyes and mouths wide open, they stared at all this money. Then their glances met, and there was a twinkle in their eyes: it would not be long before they too were just as rich.

A long, hot road now lay before them. Along the side stood kapok trees, not much more than thorny sticks, with scarcely any foliage. Their outspread branches, like scraggy arms, carried a leaf here and there, and an occasional stiff hard black fruit, from which the kapok fluff was bursting, and floating away on every unexpected gust of wind.

The men walked behind each other in silence. At first they had talked—about their little campong, about the girls, and about the paddy that was nearly ripe. But now their bodies had grown heavy. They moved their tired feet listlessly. The sweat poured down in streams from the tops of their heads, down their backs to their legs. Their throats were parched, their tongues were dry in their mouths and would not carry a word. And as they no longer talked, their thoughts also slumbered. They marched in single file along the unknown endless road. They stepped and stepped towards their fate, towards the fate of which they had no inkling. At last they reached the kotta, the town. They saw houses of stone!

"Is this the new country?" asked Ruki.

Their guide laughed contemptuously.

"Did I not tell you that you were going in a fire wagon?" he asked.

Ruki had forgotten. He said no more, and bent his head in shame before the sniggering of the other two. From under his lowered eyelids, he glanced round him stealthily. He noticed stone houses standing in the midst of cool, dark gardens, and Chinese emporiums, a whirl of colours such as he had never before seen; light, two-wheeled carriages, and a few white children.

They reached the small station. The man from

Batavia bought them a drink from a little stall. He handed each of them a glass with a red liquid made of fruit syrup and water. As they drank they experienced a new delight. But it withered under the stare of the many strangers crowded together on the benches of the station. Their faces were unknown, and their unknown voices asked: "Where do you come from?"

Ruki in a low voice mentioned the name of their campong. His heart was heavy. Suddenly he felt very lonely. Nobody knew him. He did not know where he was. None of these strangers had a name he could name. Everything familiar to him had disappeared. Only Sidin and Karimun remained, but they too sat with their faces bent to the ground. Their mouths were shut, and their eyes glanced sideways from beneath their eyelids. Then the fire wagon arrived. Ruki and his companions were startled out of their dreamy attitude, and looked terrified to see what was making this thundering noise. They moved back in terror as the long row of wagons rattled past them.

The man from Batavia pushed them into a compartment. Before they realized it, they were herded together on a wooden bench. The compartment was very full. The air was saturated with tobacco smoke and with the smell of sweating bodies. When the station-master whistled his shrill signal and the train began to move, Ruki and his friends were startled again. Fearful, they looked around at the landscape that glided past.

They went on and on. How far were they

going? To Batavia, their guide had told them. Batavia: it was but a name, a sound. The fire wagon rushed on farther and farther. Campongs, trees, rice-fields rolled by, for hours and hours.

The cadence of the wheels and the rhythmic motion made them feel sleepy. With tired, unseeing eyes they gazed straight in front of them. Their faces had become masks, without expression, without a sign of feeling behind them. They sat side by side, mute and lifeless as statues.

It was late in the afternoon when they alighted. The man from Batavia pushed them into the human stream pouring through the exit. They were swallowed by the stream as they walked after their guide without a thought of resistance. They stood in the street in a maze among the sudden hubbub of clanging carts and shouting people. They pressed close to one another, seeking protection from the unfamiliar that raged round them like a whirlpool, and threatened them on every side. The bells of the carts and the shrieking whistle of a departing train frightened them equally. They collided with foot passengers, who scolded them. Large carriages rattled past them, very close, with immense horses twice as large as the ponies to which they were accustomed. Inside sat white people. Some of them were women. They had never before seen white women. And just as they were going to cross the road they had to jump back because another fire wagon was coming towards them, one that was actually running along the street.

They went on blindly in the direction indicated

by their guide. They were too frightened now to feel admiration for him any longer as he walked completely at ease among all these dreadful machines. They had only one idea left, a frightened instinct of self-preservation. But a little later, as they passed through the newest European suburb, Karimun could not help gently nudging Ruki:

"Just look," he said, "two houses one on top of the other."

Ruki stood still in amazement at this unprecedented sight, a house with an upper storey.

"Now then, walk on," said the townsman in an imperious voice. Ruki came to himself, and hurried after the others. They had another meal in an eating place. Then their guide said: "Now you've got to listen attentively to what I'm going to say."

His voice had suddenly assumed a threatening tone, and he no longer smiled and looked friendly.

"I'm going to take you to a tuan. A tuan, just like the Controller. You know what a tuan Controller is, don't you?"

They nodded. The tuan Controller was the only European they had ever seen until to-day. Whenever something went amiss in their campong the native village chief had come with the tuan Controller. Everyone had always been rather scared of him. Rather interested in him too.

"Well now, whatever this tuan asks you, you've got to answer yes. Do you understand?"

The three of them nodded assent. They had suddenly grown a little frightened of their guide, who now led them into a low stone building. He greeted the white man who sat there with great civility, and the tuan was also very polite to him. His attitude to their guide differed considerably from that of the Controller to their native chief. This filled them with admiration.

The tuan spoke Malay. None of them knew many words of this language.

"Well, Amat, have you had a good catch?"

Amat, the man from Batavia, grinned.

"Peasant boys from a distant campong. Fools, but young and strong."

"Fine," said the European, as he moved some papers. The three of them had squatted down respectfully.

"Well," said the tuan, turning towards them, "so you want to go to Deli, to Sumatra?"

There was no reply. They did not understand the Malay spoken by the tuan.

"Don't you hear that the tuan besar is asking you something?" barked Amat.

"Yes, tuan besar," the three of them stammered in fright.

"And you are going of your own free will, aren't you?"

Under their lowered eyelids their eyes sought those of their companions in a helpless questioning. They failed to catch the meaning of the question.

"Yes," they said at last.

"You'd like to go, wouldn't you?"

There was again the same hesitation, the same silence, then: "Yes, tuan besar."

"Right!"

The tuan called a native clerk who put a paper before them and pressed a pen into their hands. They held the thing clumsily. The clerk showed them how to make a cross, and after much spilling of ink the deed was done. Then they were each handed twenty guilders. They glanced at one another and picked up the little row of silver with hesitant reverent fingers. It was merely an advance on their contract wages, and would be deducted from their future earnings to the last cent—a fact they did not realize.

The tuan again said something which they did not understand. Amat had disappeared. Two native agents belonging to the labour recruiting office pushed Ruki and his friends outside. One of them took charge of Karimun and Sidin. The other drove Ruki before him. Ruki stopped as an unconscious sign of protest.

"What's the matter with you?" snarled the agent.

"I want to go home," said Ruki very gently. The agent laughed sardonically, and pushed him on.

"Yes, yes. First you sign a contract and pocket the money and then you want to go home. Just you come along."

Ruki felt ashamed and confused. He walked on quickly, but he was not used to roughness. In the campong everyone was always friendly. There were never any quarrels, except now and again about a woman. Once this had led to murder, but that did not happen often. And nenneh of course sometimes scolded; but that was only a woman's anger and no one need take that seriously.

The agent pushed Ruki into a shed in which a number of men and women were sitting. At first, feeling awkward, he remained standing. Then, as no one took any notice of him, he squatted down on the ground. He remained like this for a long time, staring silently in front of him.

"Have they caught you too for Deli?" an older man asked him.

Ruki looked up. "They didn't catch me, Pa," he said softly.

"No, of course. You came by yourself, didn't you?" said the other scornfully. At this, the people squatting about him grinned.

"A man came into our campong, and he brought me here, Pa," explained Ruki.

"And now you're going to Sumatra. You've signed a contract?"

"Yes, Pa."

"And what do you go to seek, eh?"

Ruki hung his head. "There is cheap gold there, Pa."

The other man spat on the ground. "The dogs," he said angrily. And then to Ruki: "And you imagine that you are going to find young women there, don't you? And that you'll come back rich?"

Ruki nodded.

"Don't you believe it," said the older man. "You've got to work there. You've got to work till your body grows crooked, till your muscles ache. You've got to cut down trees, whole forests of them, and to dig the soil for the white men. That's what makes them rich. And they'll beat you and scold you. Yes. And you'll remain poor, and then you'll feel ashamed to return to your campong as a poor, wizened, worn-out coolie. And therefore you won't come back, you see? And you'll stay there for ever. I'm returning there myself, to help the other coolies. To tell them that they must not allow themselves to be beaten. That's the only reason I've signed a contract again. I don't go to look for gold."

"I won't work," said Ruki. "I want to go home. I've still got to cut grass for our buffalo." He stood up and went to the door. But a uniformed agent of the company pushed him back. "I want to go home," said Ruki. His voice was loud and insistent.

"You'd better keep your mouth shut here," said the agent threateningly.

"But I want to get out. I want to go home!" Ruki tried to push the agent on one side so that he could get past him. But the man slapped his face and said: "Now then, go back. Go and sit down where you were."

Ruki's turban had rolled off under the blow. This was an offence against custom, a thing that had never happened to him before. The blood rushed to his head.

"You mustn't beat me," he exclaimed angrily. "I won't be beaten. No one has ever beaten me before."

"Oh ho," said the agent. "If that's so, it's time you learned," and he jumped at Ruki and hit him in the face three times with his closed fist. Ruki suffered this ill usage in astonishment. Suddenly it dawned upon him that the other man was stronger, and that therefore he had authority, power, and apparently the right to strike him. He hid his face in the crook of his arm, and squatted down, thus recognizing his own inferiority.

"Mercy, Pa! Mercy!"

The agent wiped his hand. "Go back to your place, and don't come here again!"

Ashamed and humiliated, Ruki slunk away, squatted down, and gazed fixedly at the earth. A hot feeling of hatred had invaded his heart. He had never felt hatred before. There seemed to be a mist before his eyes.

"That's only the beginning," said the older man, who was sitting at his side. "You'd better do just as they tell you. It's better for you."

Ruki did not reply. He continued to stare in front of him. A dull rage began to take possession of him. It was the rage that rises only in a teased animal. But it died away with equal suddenness. His thoughts wandered towards his campong. What was nenneh doing? Was she looking for him? Where were Sidin and Karimun? He looked about in the hope of finding them, and as he did so he noticed the face of a very young woman who had seated herself opposite him. She was still almost a child. She reminded Ruki of Supinah. He saw that she was crying. She was crying very quietly and noiselessly, wiping her tears with her slendang.

"Are you also going to Deli?" asked Ruki, and suddenly he felt less lonely.

"I don't know," whispered the girl from behind the slendang which she held in front of her face.

"How did you get here?"

She did not reply, but sobbed more violently.

"Did the man from Batavia bring you here?"

She shook her head.

"Where do you come from?"

"From Buitenzorg," she said with a sob.

"Is that the name of your campong?"

She removed the slendang from before her face and looked at him. "It is a town," she said. "I was working as babu for a Dutch lady."

"But how did you come here then?"

"My brother sold me," she said, and she began to cry again.* A little later she explained: "Our buffalo died. And my father is poor. He hasn't even a rice-field. He is a carter. When he has no buffalo he can do no work. And when our buffalo died my father had not enough money to buy another one, so my brother sold me to a man who said that he would marry me and give me gold. But he did not marry me, and he did not give me gold either. He brought me here and now I do not know where he has gone. I want to go home, because my mother doesn't know where I am and because I haven't had anything to eat yet."

She began to cry once more. Ruki looked at her. She was young, and she was lovely. Her skin was pale brown, clear and gleaming. She had small hands, and her nails were reddened with henna.

*It should be remembered that only the end of this story takes place in the present time, and that this and other circumstances here narrated no longer apply. *Translators' note.*

In the heavy knot of her hair was one scented flower.

"Did the tuan give you money?" asked Ruki.

"No," she whispered, "the man took it."

Ruki remembered that he had brought some cake with him when he left home. He took it from his pocket and handed it to the young girl. Silently she took the sweet stuff and began to eat.

Then she smiled at Ruki and asked: "Do you come from Buitenzorg too?"

Ruki smiled back at her. "No," he said. "I am from a campong. It's very far from here, near a mountain."

"There are mountains near Buitenzorg too," she said with pride. "There are two of them, Gunung Salak and Gunung Gedeh."

This made them feel closer together.

"We've got a buffalo, though," said Ruki.

The young woman nodded, looked at Ruki, and asked: "What is your name?"

"Ruki."

She repeated the name. Both were silent for a moment. Then he asked: "And what is your name?"

"Karminah."

"I have got money," said Ruki, showing her the silver guilders. She looked at them.

"That man took mine away with him," she said again.

They remained close together the whole evening and throughout the night, and when, on the following morning, everyone was herded from the shed into another train, Ruki took the small bundle in which her things were done up and carried it for her. They belonged together now, and he felt that it was his duty to guard and protect her.

Step by step they shuffled along in the row of human-beings that was being led from the train to an office and from the office to the harbour. They had acquired a new name now: orang kontrak—contract hands. They moved on together, humble under the offensive title which, though it had not yet been hurled at them, they already knew to be theirs.

Neither Ruki nor Karminah spoke. All the simple things about their past which they had to tell had been told. And for the new things that were now filling them with wonder they could find no words. They had never before seen a ship, and they had never seen a harbour. Ruki, who had always lived in his campong and in the peaceful silence of the grasslands, was terrified by the noise and bustle that surrounded him. He jumped nervously on one side when men with carts, and with wheelbarrows full of wares, ran shouting past him. Often he jumped the wrong way and was rewarded by a blow, or he hurt himself against protruding bales. Then he merely invoked Allah.

"Lah-illah-il-Allah!"

The rattle of the cranes and the thud with which cargoes were dumped into ships' holds, the shouts, the hurry, the shrieks of the sirens, the hoarse moan of the steam whistles—all this chaos and frantic confusion filled him with fear.

He walked on with deafened ears and blinded eyes.

He understood nothing, and made no attempt to understand. He only knew that nothing here resembled the happenings in his campong. But he was no longer in his campong, and that explained everything.

By his side walked Karminah. She walked with lowered head and downcast eyes. She had modestly drawn her slendang across her small breasts. When a heavily loaded cart jogged past her, she shrank together and gripped his hand. But Ruki himself was so confused that he did not notice this.

They were driven up the gangway with curses and blows, like a herd of cattle. A very long queue of contract coolies was being embarked. Under their half-closed eyelids their glances shot out threateningly. Their heads and shoulders were hunched up like those of animals afraid of being beaten. There was rebellion in their fear, but no one heeded it, for they were weak. They were orang kontrak, sold body and soul.

The women uttered shrill, hysterical yells as they were driven up the steep gangway. Sometimes they clung to the side rope or gripped each other by the arm. But a stern word from one of their conductors or from a sailor made them move on. The waist of the ship was full of contract coolies. At last the gangway was pulled in and the heavy steam whistle resounded across the harbour. A shiver ran through the whole ship. Very slowly the quayside receded.

"But we're going away from land!" exclaimed Karminah in terror. Ruki's mouth fell open. He had foreseen this as little as had Karminah. He had not realized why they had been made to go on board the ship. He had not wondered about it either, simply because he had given no thought to the matter. He stood close to the rail and looked down into the murky water that separated the ship from the pier. A curious sensation came to his head. It reeled. Was it because for the first time in his life the ground was unsteady under his feet? Or was there a greater emotion that stirred him though his heart did not understand it?

Karminah took a corner of her slendang in her mouth. Her eyes stared, wide open and vacant. She seemed more than ever an anxious child that had lost its way.

The contract coolies stood shoulder to shoulder, mutely gazing at the land that moved farther and farther away, and eyeing the sea that surrounded the whole ship. Suddenly from the silent crowd rose a woman's cry: "My child! my child! I have left my child behind, and now we are going away!"

She pulled at her hair, she bit her arms, she tore open her jacket, she shrieked and yelled. Those about her drew a little away from her, leaving a space around her. She threw herself upon the deck and banged her head on the wooden planks.

A sailor from Madura pushed his way through the crowd. He was half a head smaller than the Javanese and Sundanese coolies, but his shoulders were well set up and his whole sturdy body proclaimed its strength. His dark face was stern. "What's all this noise?" he demanded in a stentorian voice.

The contract coolies shrank back nervously at the sight of him.

"What's all this?" he demanded again, bending down towards the woman. He shook her by the shoulders, but the only result was that she began to yell more loudly.

From the bridge the captain shouted angrily: "Why the deuce don't you keep order there?"

"Shut up!" shouted the sailor from Madura. But the woman continued to yell. A Javanese came forward. He addressed the sailor respectfully with the title of elder:

"Abang, she has forgotten her child, and now the devil has taken hold of her."

"So that's it," said the sailor with a grin. He tucked up his sleeves, and bent over the woman again. "Do you hear me?" he shouted. "Shut up, or I'll beat you!"

The woman bit and kicked around her, but the sailor seized her by the knot of her hair, lifted her head up a little, and gave her a blow with his closed fist full in the face. She screamed loudly. There was some commotion among the men.

"Do not beat her, abang!" the Javanese said. "Let her cry! She has forgotten her child, and now the devil has come into her. It is not her fault."

"Mind your own business," replied the sailor, pushing the Javanese on one side. "And you . . . will you be quiet or not?" He kicked the woman and shook her. She stopped shrieking, but began to cry and sob.

"Stop that too," the sailor ordered her. He held

his fist ready for another blow. The woman shrank together and was silent. With a threatening scowl, his vicious face close to hers, he looked at her. "Sit up," he said. She got up and squatted down. "Close your jacket. You're too old to show your naked breast."

Full of confusion, she readjusted her clothes. Some of the men round her were grinning, and the women, hiding their faces behind their slendangs, giggled in secret. They got so much enjoyment out of the opportunity of laughing at someone being mocked that it killed all feelings of pity in them.

"Tidy your hair!"

She knotted it with one turn of the wrist so that it stuck in position without the aid of a pin.

The sailor put his hands in his pockets. He expanded his chest. He felt infinitely above these stupid campong dwellers who allowed themselves to be carried like cattle to Sumatra. He looked down at the woman again. She was still squatting. Silent now, she stared in front of her. Tears flowed from her eyes. She was crying without sobbing, without uttering a sound. Her hands lay folded in her lap, and tears trickled down upon them. She sat like this for three days till they reached Deli, and she never moved. She did not eat or drink, she did not sleep. She did not wipe away the tears. Nobody paid any attention to her. There were others who had left a child behind them, or a wife or a husband. Many had not taken leave of father or mother. They had left house and rice-field, and had no idea what was going to happen to them. They were ignorant of the fate towards which the ship was carrying them.

The sailor pushed his way through the contract coolies. He stopped in front of Ruki and Karminah. He looked at Karminah. She was the only young and good-looking woman among the new coolies for Sumatra. Unashamed, he inspected her delicate face, her narrow almond-shaped eyes, her eyebrows that seemed to have been drawn with a brush above them, her flat nose and her small full mouth. He looked at the curve of her young breasts whose lovely form was revealed through her slendang, at her hips, at her very slender waist, and at the small feet that appeared beneath her sarong. He took her by the arm.

"Come along."

But Ruki stood up before him, facing him. "She is my wife," he said. "She must stay here."

The sailor looked contemptuously at Ruki. "What do you want, you contract dog? You've no say here. The woman is coming with me."

"But she is my wife," shouted Ruki, while the blood rushed to his temples and blinded him.

The man from Madura laughed. He gave Ruki a slap in the face, and pulled Karminah away with him. Ruki saw her disappear in the crowd, and caught a glimpse of her face as she looked round, and of her eyes, large and frightened, imploring his help.

Every day he waited for her to return, but he did not see her again until they came to Deli. With fatalistic resignation he thought: "What can I do?

The other man is stronger. He has power. He can shout and beat. But I am only orang kontrak." It was fate, and Allah had sent it. Thus far did his thoughts go, and then he stared before him, without thought, waiting for the day when maybe the ship would touch land somewhere. He did not know what would come then. He did not think of it either.

Three days passed like this. Ruki was startled by a gentle touch. Karminah was at his side again. She looked ill and had grown thin. She squatted down near him in silence. They sat together like this for a long while; she said nothing and he asked nothing. Then, from the scarf that was wound round her waist, she took a few cigarettes and gave them to Ruki. Without saying a word, he accepted them and lit one of them. He knew, of course, that she had been given the cigarettes by the sailor, but he also knew the meaning of the right of the stronger.

"Did he beat you too?" he asked at last.

"When I did not do what he wanted me to, he beat me, of course. I'm only orang kontrak now."

Ruki nodded. "All orang kontrak are beaten," he said resignedly. Then he pointed, and said: "There is land."

She gazed across the water that flashed back the sharp sunlight.

"Perhaps we are going to leave the ship now," said Ruki. But she replied only: "Lah-illah-il-Allah!"

There was a long silence between them. Then she said: "I have been ill. The sea made me drunk. Were you not ill?"

"I was not," said Ruki, and it seemed to him a matter of course, for was he not a man?

When the ship had stopped and had moored alongside the small jetty, the contract coolies were taken ashore. They stood all in a bunch like a herd of frightened cattle. They saw nothing of their surroundings, but pushed close together, starting every now and then, and seeking shelter behind each other's bodies. Now and then they cast a sidelong glance at the ship that had brought them; it was now the only known thing in this strange environment, in this new land.

Behind and round the steamer were Chinese junks. On the smooth, shiny, swelling surface of the water they swayed almost imperceptibly. Grotesque as the wings of bats, their sails were spread against a rigid expanse of sky that had no clouds. Flat upon the sea as though they were so much foam sat narrow praws, dreamy in the hot tropical day.

The low muddy shore rested upon the water like a threshold. From the dark brown mud palm trees and mangroves shot up. But none of these new things was observed by the coolies. They perceived only the thundering noise of the shaking cranes, the clatter of the hand-carts that passed close by them, the shouts of the half-naked Chinese porters, the shrill whistles of the men who directed the unlading of the cargo. They had no inkling of what was to happen to them, and they gave no thought to the matter. Their thoughts, caught in the same narrow circle that encompassed their bodies, did nothing but shrink in passive resistance from the terrifying din that overwhelmed them. Brief words of command shook them from their dazed impassivity, and drove them to the quarantine station, where the men were separated from the women. Now Ruki thought that he had been finally separated from Karminah; but a few days later he met her again: she was put into the same railway compartment as he.

"Eh, Karminah!"

He was so glad to see her that a smile glanced over his face, and he seized her hand for a moment; but he allowed it to slip away again. Karminah giggled, and buried her head in the corner of her slendang, hiding even her eyes. Then, with their faces closed once more and expressionless, they sat down on the wooden bench. They looked up only when they were startled into attention by the Bengali superintendent who was making a tour of inspection to verify that none of the new coolies had escaped.

At the small stations at which they stopped during the journey they were able to buy food. Ruki paid for Karminah, who had no money. While they ate, they paid no attention to the landscape. They did not notice that they were passing through tobacco plantations, and that this country was altogether different from their own. It was only when the virgin forest swallowed them that Ruki took in the picture.

The virgin forest grew out of a gurgling swamp. Live trees, dying trees, dead trees, all of them gigantic, were strangled in the close embrace of fiercely growing creepers that stifled them and sucked the life out of them, but held them erect in a close unrelenting grip even when they were dead.

The dead trunks and the bare knotty branches stood in a dense mass, and the creepers climbed towards the naked crowns of the trees that rose like skeletons high above the hot, spongy soil; and from the crowns the creepers hung down again in festoons, gripping one another, interwoven like nests full of serpents. It was a fantastic mixture of life stifled and murdered, of life passionate, violent, and intense, rising again and again from the pitiless destruction that encompassed it.

Sometimes, at the extreme tip of a bare branch, a bird of prey sat with its spying head bent downward like an image of waiting death in lofty loneliness above this furious but silent struggle of living and dying things. Higher still than the cynical spying bird hung the measureless dome of the sky, of the tropical sun-drenched sky, towards which shimmering heat rose from the sweltering morass.

Ruki looked at all these things. The others also looked.

"It's the rimbu," said some of them. Then the others without the slightest display of interest in their faces said: "Ts . . . eh! It's the rimbu."

Ruki sat in silence at Karminah's side. He had tucked his legs up beneath him, and crossed them under him. His eyes were cast down. He did not speak. He did not smoke. He had ceased to eat. A strange, deadly silence was growing in the depths of his being, and held him enveloped in a haze of meditation. It was a veil that swathed even his thoughts. Was he thinking of his campong, of his nenneh, of their buffalo? Was he comparing the melancholy solitude of this country, of this forbidding sombre forest, with the beautiful loneliness of the sunny grasslands of his own land where the only shadow was that of the fertilizing clouds?

Sitting straight up, his legs crossed, his delicate, weak hands folded in his lap, his head bent forward just a little, he remained there in placid immobility: he might have been a prophet who had withdrawn from the whirl of the fancied external world into the narrow circle of total passivity.

His pale brown face, utterly void of expression, had become a thin mask of high, aristocratic beauty. Under his forehead the lines of the nose, broad but not coarse, sloped down; the full bow of his mouth separated the pure line of his cheeks from that of his chin. His downcast eyelids seemed two petals subtle as those of a dark red rose. But the wonder of his face lay in the eyes. The motionless pupils were set in tenderly outlined openings, very narrow slits that slanted slightly upwards towards the outer corners. Something of his deeply mystic soul seemed trying to escape through these fissures. It seemed to tremble, an ethereal drop, from the long lashes. But the fragile, shell-like eyelids held it back, and it was as though this passive, pure, this kindly face reflected a sort of shadow of external events which caused a gentle, imperceptible smile to play round the corners of the mouth—a smile that was there, and yet not there.

How came it, then, that this face was so appallingly like the world around it? How was it that under this gossamer veil of still reflection, within this nothingness of passivity, there existed an undefined but very different image composed of a mixture of resistance and murder? How was it possible that this delicate, expressionless mask bore the signs of passionate life? In its invisible smile there was an echo of the pensive spying of the bird of prey, and of the lofty blue ideal of the vaulted sky. Escaping, yet restrained, here too was the soul of the melancholy tree slowly done to death by the poisonous creeper.

How was it that Ruki's features carried the traces of all this, betrayed it, and yet remained so quiet, so stonily motionless in this unreal smile, this intangible, deeply mystical bliss? . . .

Perhaps it was because from the depths of his inexplicable being silence, strange and deathlike, grew up heavily scented and poisonous as a flower of the swamp, but white as a soul that is pure, hiding the mystery of his spirit in its sweet white perfume.

Then, infinitely tired, his dreamy eyes looked up. Large and dark, they took in the landscape.

Gold . . . Women . . . Adventure. . . . These were the promises of the stranger. What had become of them? He had found only blows, violence, loneliness. He thought of his campong. Of nenneh, of the paddy that was ripening and should have been cut. He thought of the river and of the evening prayer. But while he thought of these things, his hands continued to rest in his lap. He did not turn rebel. He just sat there. He knew that the pain in his heart was homesickness, but what could he do about it? He had no idea how he could have resisted the power that had overcome him. He was orang kontrak. He had sold his soul. Perhaps it was all the will of Allah. Who could tell?

The train carried him on. He knew not whither. He did not know what life would give him. He did not know what it would ask. What, in any case, was life? He did not know, he did not wonder.

He had been in the train for two hours. Evening was falling. The light that entered the compartment had grown red, and now it was greyish. Shadows hung round those who sat at even a short distance from him. When he looked around him, he could see only Karminah. Karminah reminded him of Supinah, and Supinah made him think of the river.

"I have not yet bathed," he remarked.

"Neither have I," she answered quietly. Her eyes continued to rest on her hands, which lay in her lap.

"And it is evening already," he said.

"It is growing dark," she replied, and she lifted up her head to look through the little window. To Ruki she was now only a dim outline.

Inside the dark room that was rushing on and on towards an end known to none of them silence was growing. They were all depressed. They had said all they had to say about the few things they had to talk about. Sometimes one of them yawned aloud, and this made the others grin. But silence returned above the rhythmic sound of the wheels. The atmosphere was close with heat and the odour of human bodies.

Suddenly the train stopped. There was a long,

shrill whistle. Several resounding shocks. A hiss as the engine let off steam. Then there was utter quiet. They were startled out of the quietude and told that they must alight: they had reached the end of the railway.

In the midst of the virgin forest stood a small open shed. The rails came to a dead end. Thus far had western technique broken its way through prehistoric nature. It had crept on a hundred miles or so through the dense growth of the mighty wilderness. But here the forest was as yet undefeated, and in the immense living silence the train, which had suddenly ceased its panting, became an insignificant, dead thing. It was unimportant, man-made, overwhelmed by the dark majesty of the forest that encircled both train and terminus in the thousandfold threat of its massive vigour. The shining steel railroad, the work of human hands, became a ridiculous, puny attempt at blasphemy.

The Bengali was still acting as supervisor. He counted the coolies, and saw that they carried with them their little bits of luggage. Bewildered and uncertain like a herd of lost animals, they stood there on the dark platform which was sparingly lit by a small oil lamp. They looked round them and shivered, and asked each other where they were; but none was able to answer.

They spent the night in the station. Those who had little mats stretched themselves out on them. The others sat down on the wooden benches in the shed. As they slept, they fell against one another. They struck at the mosquitoes that came in their millions from the forest and from the swamp; and their confused dreams were penetrated by the dark sounds of the forest.

They awoke in the morning stiff and tired. They bought food from the little station stall—fruit and small portions of rice wrapped in banana leaves. Almost all of them still had money left from the advances they had received, and those who had not borrowed from those who had. They fraternized and called each other "suderah kappal"—shipmate. All they knew of one another was the place from which they had come. There were Sundanese from the high plateau, and from the mountains of the Preanger Regencies. There were Bantams from western Java and Javanese from the centre and east of Java. They spoke different languages. Many of them knew hardly a word of Malay, that Esperanto of the Dutch East Indies, and were therefore unable to converse. But there was among them one bond of union: the ship. And one common future linked them together: the contract. Body and soul, they had sold themselves for three years to the company that had need of their muscles. They had lost their will, their freedom, their rights. They were a new people without fatherland, without family, without tradition: they were orang kontrak.

Orang kontrak! They were the humble men who carried in their ignorant servile hands the first stones of a new evolution.

The Bengali made them form a long procession two abreast. They began to walk. They walked, walked, walked, along a narrow footpath through the forest. The slippery mud stuck between the widespread toes of their broad, bare feet. Chattering monkeys looked at them inquisitively. Hornbills flew across their path with heavy wing-beats. On both sides of them was the quiet hush of the virgin forest, where the trees stood fifteen and twenty times as tall as they. In this narrow tunnel through the forest hung a cool damp shade. They went on in silence. They did not know whither. They did not know how far. And they did not know why.

They walked on through the strange land. On their heads they carried the small bundles that held all they possessed. Sweat poured down their backs. They hurt their bare feet and made them bleed against the stones that lay in their way. They scratched themselves on the thorny branches that straggled across the path.

Ruki walked by Karminah's side and carried her little bundle. Once she said: "I'm thirsty." He felt in his pocket and found a lime, which he handed to her. Later she said: "I want to go home," but to this he made no reply.

During the afternoon they reached a river. There was no bridge—only a ferry. But they could not cross because there had been rain in the mountains, and the narrow river rushed past furiously between its steep overgrown banks. Pieces of wood, stakes of houses, branches, and banana stems were carried down by the boiling brown stream in its wild career.

They spent the night by the side of the river. It was a queer camp. Those who had a mat spread it out on the ground. The rest squatted down and slept as best they could. But first they bathed, cautiously dipping water in tins and in pails from the raging stream. Some of them afterwards turned their faces to Mecca and said their prayer, first standing humbly with their hands against their faces, then bending and sinking down in kneeling attitudes to kiss the soil. For even here the soil must have been created by Allah.

Next day about noon the ferry carried them over the subsiding waters.

III

THE new contract coolies squatted down in long rows in front of the manager's little office on the fringe of the teak plantation. They squatted and waited. In the warm, heavy stillness of the day their silence hung like something even heavier. From time to time they peeped shyly from below their eyelids at the bare wooden buildings, and then at the closed, waiting faces of the others in the long row.

Only from inside the building came sounds, sounds that were brief, violent, frightening. There was the voice of a European angrily scolding a clerk. The heavy lid of an iron chest was closed with a bang. A ruler fell clattering from the table to the wooden floor. Then again there was the voice demanding an explanation in a loud, imperious tone. It was as though all the unknown danger, all the menace of this new, strange life was concentrated within the thin wooden walls of the manager's little office. It seemed to seep through the open windows and doors out into the sunny, peaceful, tropical afternoon.

Behind the coolies lay the teak plantation. From the tall slender trees a large leaf now and then detached itself and spun gently down to the ground. A hen was scratching under the fallen leaves, looking for worms and small frogs for her cheeping chicks. On the path in front of the office a dog slumbered. Sometimes one of its ears twitched, as though it were dreaming. Squatting against a pole was the office orderly, gazing indifferently and sleepily in front of him.

Suddenly the silent menace inside the little building assumed life and size. A European had appeared at the window. He filled the whole space with his bulk, with his coarse, red, puffed-up face, his broad, white-clad shoulders, and his heavy round stomach that overhung the window sill.

"Mandur besar!" he shouted.

The coolies shrank together, in an effort to escape from the power that issued from this European.

"Yes, tuan besar!"

Hurriedly, but without making a sound, the head mandur approached from somewhere behind the building.

"Go through the goods of these new hands with the clerk."

"Yes, tuan besar."

The figure disappeared. Its place was taken by the Malay clerk, who was small and graceful. He began to ask the names and the place of origin of each of the coolies in turn. The same question, posed monotonously time after time, and the brief replies punctuated the silence like a succession of stones dropped into a pool. Sometimes the colloquy was in Javanese, sometimes in Sundanese. Sometimes no reply was forthcoming. Then the clerk repeated his question in a louder voice, and the man addressed would answer softly with his name. Some of them at that moment assumed a new name: it was a quiet and tragic acceptance of their fate. This silent breach with their past was their sole meek expression of resistance to their future.

"Open your bundles and boxes!"

Though surprised, they obediently did as they were told. The men showed no hesitation, but the women held back. Some of them tried to hide things of which they were ashamed.

"Now then."

Giggling because she was embarrassed, Karminah undid her bundle with lingering fingers. Her whole property lay exposed—a broken comb, a fragment of mirror, the withered flower which she had once worn in her hair, and which still gave out a whiff of stale perfume, a crumpled undervest, a flowered cotton vest, and a rolled up sarong.

"What's in this kaïn?" asked the head mandur harshly.

"Nothing, Pa. It's just a dirty kaïn."

"Let me see."

"But . . ."

"Let me see, I say. Unroll it."

The head mandur prodded the sarong with his stick. She hesitated a moment longer. Then, her head lowered in shame, she opened the cloth.

"You can fold it up."

"Yes, Pa."

She said it very softly. The other women were giggling around her. The men looked down at the ground, hurt at the offence to the modesty of a woman. It was a feeling they had not yet learned to overcome.

"Knives? Creeses? Has anyone got any?"

The men were searched bodily. Their hidden weapons were taken away from them. At last they were left in peace, and they sat down again, silent and submissive, waiting for what was to come next. And again it was as though all the chances of their new destiny centred in the little office, inside those four walls where decisions were being taken about them.

As they waited, they began to comprehend something of their situation. There was one centre of power: the office of the tuan besar. And there was one central supreme power: the tuan besar himself. That together they were stronger than the one white man was a thought that never crossed their minds. Between them and this idea stood the barrier of a primitive, irrational fear.

It was growing late. Shadows were creeping out of the teak plantation. The light was losing its colour. The silence weighed more heavily. Then, suddenly, into the midst of the silence fell a few harsh sounds. Within the four fateful walls a clock chimed hastily, penetratingly. It was half-past five. The office orderly awoke from his stupor, stood up, and with the back of an old hatchet banged on a piece of rail, half consumed by rust, that was suspended in front of the office. He beat very fast, with short, resounding blows. Gradually he beat more slowly. Then there was a pause and one final blow. It was half-past five, the end of the day's labour. From the distance, in five different directions, resounded the same kind of bangs. It was a sudden rising flood of echoes in the stilly atmosphere. Then followed other sounds—the voices of hundreds of coolies. They were talking in loud, clipped Chinese words, dull, shapeless Javanese, high-pitched, melodious Sundanese.

Then the coolies passed by. They were nearly all of them Javanese or Sundanese. One of their compounds was not far from the office. They lived in complete segregation from the Chinese: for between compound and kongsee lay, like a deep chasm, the irreconcilable difference of two Eastern religions.

They jogged past, long lines of tired figures. Over their shoulders they carried their spades. Dark brown, almost black were their naked bodies which laboured every day for ten hours under the relentless glare of the sun, and on their dark bodies, as on the bodies of the dark buffaloes, stuck the drying mud in greyish streaks.

Some of the men who passed left the line and came towards the office, where they squatted down and waited. They were men upon whose lean bodies hard work had developed the muscle. They sat a little apart from the new coolies, and now and then cast a stealthy glance at the newcomers, looking at the women as though they were counting their number.

"What do you men want?" demanded the head mandur brusquely.

One of the coolies rose, took a few steps towards

the head mandur, and squatted again. "I ask for a woman, mandur besar."

"What is your name?"

"Sentono, Pa. I have already served six years' contract, but I have no woman yet."

"Only fifteen women have come."

"So I see, Pa. But if the mandur besar will have pity on me, and if it pleases him to allot me a woman, then I ask for a woman, Pa."

The head mandur reflected a moment. "Right," he said then. He knew that this coolie would, silently and without the assistant's knowledge, give him a part of his wages in payment for the woman. He turned towards the new coolies, pointed to the first woman he set eyes on, and said: "You can take that woman." She was carrying a child, a little boy, in her slendang. Then, turning towards the woman, he said: "What is your name?"

"Wirio."

"Get up and follow this man."

Hesitatingly she stood up. Without looking at her, Sentono murmured: "Thank you, Pa." He went quietly towards the compound. The woman followed him without a word. Much the same thing happened to the other old hands, except in the case of one young coolie who had stopped with the older men.

"What are you doing here, Nur?"

The coolie, a young Javanese, looked ahead with hostile eyes. "I must have a woman," he said abruptly.

"*Must* have a woman?" repeated the head mandur. "Why must? You can't give orders here, do you see?" He bent down towards the coolie, pinched the lobe of his ear between his thumb and finger, and repeated: "Must, must you? Must, must you? What do you want, you son of a pig?"

Nur tried to free himself. "I ask for a woman," he said. "I have been here a year."

The head mandur looked down at him sarcastically, and pushed him so that instead of squatting he fell down on the ground. Nur resumed his previous attitude. Again the mandur pushed him and made him lose his balance. Once more Nur picked himself up, and once more the head mandur, pushing him in the face and by the shoulder, made him fall over.

"What do you want with a woman? What do you want with a woman? Others have been here for five years, for seven years even, and have no woman. What do you think, you son of a dog? Do you imagine you'll be given a woman at once? You will have to wait ten times one year. You monkey, you dog, you buffalo!"

Nur looked up with hatred in his eyes. His whole face was a threat. But the head mandur pushed his face down. "Squat, and quickly, or I'll give you such a beating! Do you understand me? Look round you. There are thirty men here waiting for a woman. Do you see? And there are three hundred more in the compound. . . ."

Nur made no reply. The head mandur landed a big blow in his face. "Do you see?" he shouted.

"Yes."

"And now have a look at the new coolies. How many women are left among them?"

"Only one," mumbled Nur.

"Well, if that's so . . . You can get along home. Now then, off with you!"

Nur stood up, muttering vaguely, threw his spade resentfully over his shoulder, and disappeared into the rapidly gathering dusk.

Ruki watched all this anxiously. The one woman who remained was Karminah. And sure enough she was given to an old Javanese named Marto, a coolie from section one.

"Now then, you there, follow him!"

The head mandur pushed her by the shoulder. She hesitated and cast a glance at Ruki. Ruki stood up and squatted humbly before the head mandur.

"Why must she go with Marto, Pa?"

"Because Marto was promised a woman long ago," said the head mandur.

"But she is my wife, Pa!"

"Coolies have no wives here," shouted the head mandur. "Go back to your place."

"She is my wife, Pa. She must stay with me."

Ruki got no reply. But Marto nudged Karminah. "Now then, come along."

The blood rushed to Ruki's head. Impulsively he groped for his knife. But it had been taken away from him.

"She is my wife!" he repeated in a threatening voice. He was standing straight up now before the head mandur, like a man who is defending his rightful property.

The head mandur looked at him menacingly. "Go back to your place!"

"I won't!"

"You . . . won't?" asked the head mandur, taking a step towards him. "You . . . won't? That's not the way to speak here. You could say won't in your campong, but here you can't. 'I won't' are no words for a contract dog . . ."

He seized Ruki's upper arm. Ruki tried to wrench himself loose. The other man suddenly slapped him full in the face.

"Oh . . ." shouted Ruki, rubbing the place, which was flushing a vague red beneath his brown skin. The head mandur lifted his rattan cane, and brought it down with a bang on Ruki's skull.

"Oh . . ." shouted Ruki again. "Mercy, Pa!"

"Oh, so. Then you've learnt at last how things go here. Be quiet and go back to your place."

Stooping, almost crawling, he returned to his place in the line of coolies. Karminah had already disappeared.

The head mandur called the under mandurs, and with the assistance of the clerk he distributed the new coolies over the different sections. Ruki was drafted to section three, under mandur Amat.

"Have you still so much to say for yourself?" asked mandur Amat, in a threatening voice. The other coolies grinned. Ruki bowed his head in shame.

"No, Pa."

"That's wise. . . . For I have a stick too. Look at it!"

The others grinned again.

"Get along with you. . . !"

In silence Ruki joined the others. The mandur conducted them to the compound of section three, where he allotted rooms and sleeping places to them.

## IV

IT was evening, and the new arrivals in section three were surrounded by a circle of old coolies who were asking about life in Java. They sat in the empty, shabby square in the centre of the compound. It seemed like a dark, gaping void from which the gaming shed rose like a dark silhouette sending up its pointed roof to the bright, star-lit sky. Ruki was squatting down, listening to the questions and to the answers. Java. . . . The word lived in all the questions, in all the replies with its deep significant sound.

This open space was just like the campong square, thought Ruki, but it was larger, much larger. And there were no houses. . . . He looked around him. Under their long, palm thatched roof, the tiny huts that were the coolie dormitories stood in long rows forming the sides of a rectangle. From inside came the vague glow of reddish lamps. On the covered footway in front of the little huts a few women were sitting. At the far end of the square some coconut palms threw up their thin slender trunks close to the two wells that were hidden behind a bamboo hedge.

The senior coolies told of their existence, of the hard work in the forest and in the swamp. They described how they were beaten by the tuan, and how the mandurs thrashed them too. All one could do was to be very careful and do precisely as one was told.

"And . . . is one really allowed to gamble?"

"Oh yes. . . . Gamble!"

Their eyes lighted up. They smoked in silence, pensively, and as they thought about gambling their eyes grew intense and covetous. A hush fell around them, now that their voices no longer filled the space —a hush that seemed to creep on from the darkness of the forest over the empty compound. Curtains of smoke hung round the huts. Everywhere glowed smouldering bonfires of grass. Through the hush broke the occasional splash of water as someone let down a pail into one of the wells, and poured water over himself. Listening to this sound of bathing, Ruki's vague mind conjured up the dim memory of Supinah's image, and Supinah's image melted into Karminah's.

"Where is section one?" he asked the coolie by his side. The coolie pointed away into the darkness.

"Over there. An hour's walk towards the north. Why?"

"My wife is there," answered Ruki.

"Were you married in Java then?"

Ruki shook his head. "No. I was with her in the shed in Java and later on board the ship."

"Is she young?"

Ruki did not answer at once.

"Yes, she is still young," he said at last. "The head mandur gave her to Marto, but I won't have it."

The other chuckled drily. "Won't have it? What won't you have? She's a contract coolie, and so are you. What can you do? If you won't have a thing, you get beaten, and if the head mandur had not allotted her, she would probably have been taken by the tuan. That is, if she's good-looking."

"Which tuan? The tuan besar?"

"Oh, one of the tuans. . . . Perhaps the tuan besar."

Ruki thought of the tuan besar, of the office, and of the mysterious power that pervaded the place. It was the power of the white man.

He bowed his head. Dark thoughts whirled through his brain. Somewhere there was a hazy idea of revenge. His heart began to beat irregularly. Through his blood a hot sensation rushed.

Hati panas. . . .

He had heard those words in his childhood now and then. When a man went hati panas he sat for days stolidly brooding over an insult. Fascinated and frightened at the same time, the women whispered around him. Sometimes there was a fight. Once there was murder. Then the Controller and the police had come. A man had been taken away, and he had never come back. Nobody knew what had happened to him.

"He has been hanged," some people said, "hanged." But no one knew what this meant exactly. None of them had ever seen such a thing.

Muffled sounds fell on the still evening. They interrupted Ruki's heated thoughts. The old coolies rose.

"What are you doing?" asked the newcomers in surprise.

"We must sleep now, it is nine. Do you not hear the beating of the ton-tong?" They pointed to a little shed in which hung a hollow tree trunk. One of the coolies was beating it. The sound of the blows was wafted over the compound, and a moment later the ton-tongs of the other four sections could be heard. The sounds melted together, crossed each other, and died away against the fringe of the forest, sending out unexpected echoes through the murmuring tropic night. Then there was silence again, and the silence suddenly lent a great harshness to the voices of the coolies. A child cried loudly and began to shriek. High above its voice came the scolding of an angry woman.

"Off with you to bed!" shouted a mandur, and the men all obeyed. Ruki shared a room with five other single men. It was a small square hut. It had four rough walls and a dusty earthen floor. The walls, covered with dust and soot, were made of rough boards which the plane had scarcely touched. Six narrow couches stood by the walls. On five of them lay a tikar—a fibre mat.

"You have no tikar yet?" one of the coolies asked Ruki.

"No."

"And no pillow?"

"No."

"Pay day will be in ten days. Then you can buy all you need. There will be a Chinese stall in the compound at which you can buy things."

"Yes."

A little lamp was left burning. Around it was a circle of flickering light, beyond which the shadows crept darkly through the hut. Rats ran along the roof, chasing each other, squeaking and scurrying about.

"Where is Kromorejo?" Ruki heard someone ask in the dark.

They all grinned. At last someone said: "He will be here in a moment. He has gone to fetch Isah."

"Is she sleeping with him to-night?"

"Yes. He has still got money. He was lucky in the gaming shed last hari besar."

The wooden door was opened carefully, just enough to allow two figures to slip through. A woman's suppressed giggles penetrated the silence. Then a man's voice was heard muttering.

Ruki drew up his legs. He was lying on his side, one hand under his head. Just opposite him was Kromorejo's couch. Dimly in the glimmer of the oil lamp he could see two figures lying side by side. He listened to their whispering voices and to the woman's occasional giggle.

He understood one word: gold. There was a moment's silence.

"A small gold coin, or a large one?" asked the woman.

"A large one."

The woman was silent. She no longer giggled. Her whole being was pervaded by breathless adoration of the gold she was to receive. This adoration hung heavy in the heavy atmosphere. The others felt it too. All of them in the darkness thought of one thing: "Mas . . . gold!"

So it was true after all, thought Ruki in his dull, tired brain. There was gold, and one was allowed to gamble. But women. . . . He heard the couch creaking. Almost unconsciously he listened . . .

He struck out at a mosquito that was humming round his ear. A little later he fell asleep. He did not notice Isah's going—she went without a sound.

## V

AT five o'clock, while it was still dark, the ton-tong roused the coolies from their deep sleep. They awakened moaning and yawning, stretched themselves and scratched. During the night they had been bitten by bugs and mosquitoes. Some of them washed, bending over tins of water in front of the huts. Others merely rinsed their mouths and changed from a sarong into a pair of shorts. Then, when the ton-tong sounded again and all the other ton-tongs sent back an echo, they took their spades on their shoulders and walked to work slowly, sleepily, reluctantly. They always marched in single file, dark silhouettes moving through the dark day-break. Above their heads the stars paled on the greyish sky, and disappeared before the deepening glow coming up from the east. All around them on the distant horizon, encompassed by the virgin forest, half enveloped still in the milk-white morning mists, was land that would one day become the new estate. It was a colourless, dead plain where everything that had once been alive had been uprooted, burned, destroyed. There had been the stately trees of the ancient forest, the thorny rattan, the creeping, stifling weeds, the ferns and the mosses, the snow-white and dark purple orchids that had exhaled their perfume unseen. There had been animals too—

serpents, scorpions, ants, and centipedes. They had crawled, wriggled, worked, and reproduced in the hot, putrefying weeds, decaying wood, and detritus of all kinds. Continually a life just ended had risen again, pushing, murdering and throttling other life, striving upwards towards the glimpses of sunlight that filtered down between the high crowns of the trees like drops of melting copper. For centuries on end the secret struggle for life had gone on in the perennial dusk. Suddenly men had come, cutting, uprooting, destroying the majestic tree trunks, and the myriad suckers of the creepers. The blows of axes had resounded through the forest, and a thundering roar, magnified a thousandfold, had echoed through the dim depths like the sound of a dire disaster as these old giants of the forest fell dying. Still, under these colossal trunks with foliage lying criss-cross all over the ground, the black, soft, moist humus had continued to live. While the trunks and the branches of the trees were dying, the tough, juicy creepers and parasites had continued to grow and prosper. Ferns had shot up, orchids had flowered with a last magnificent efflorescence from the bark that was crumbling away. Deep under this chaos of leaves and fibres, creeping creatures still lived, unaware as yet that death was rioting above them.

Then in one morning at one stroke fire had put an end to all that remained. It had flared up, crackling, hissing, sizzling among the mighty tree trunks. It had greedily devoured and digested the things of the forest that had remained untouched for centuries. It had stretched its thousand contorted arms towards the blue sky where the brassy sun was less consuming than itself. There had been a raging sea of fire, a furious flood of flames bellowing as it reached up heavenward. Before they had realized what was happening, plants and animals had been annihilated. For one second they had been checked in their accustomed ways. Then they had perished, destroyed utterly by the ruddy fire.

By night, nothing had been left but a smouldering, smoking mass of débris, a black, hot world of ashes and soot and mangled fragments. All that remained of the river of flames was a thin deposit of greyish dust. Tiny tongues of fire licked the corpses of the trees, and crept along bits of trunk that had escaped the full fury of the fire. The evening breeze carried away thin strips of calcinated grass and fern and dropped them in the form of a tenuous black dust. Then the wind freshened and blew on the smouldering stumps until the fire blazed up again and, though satiated, began to feed once more, devouring the last remnants of its vast banquet. Sometimes the smouldering heaps crumbled together with a dull, tragic thud or with a last tired sigh. Then a shower of sparks rose up into the air and dropped asunder, like red stars chased across a landscape by the wind.

One tree remained standing isolated in the ill-used plain, a mighty trunk whose crown had been merely singed. The axe spared it henceforth, as the fire had done. It was the most sacred of all sacred trees, the king tree. Its white stem, so many centuries old, alarmed the coolies. They dared not touch the tree that could be destroyed by Allah alone.

Lofty and pure, it contemplated alike the destruction and the construction wrought by human hands —mighty in themselves, but puny in comparison with the strength of the sacred tree.

Barren, empty, desolate, overpowered and humbled, the land lay there, waiting patiently for the yoke of civilization. Chinese were turning the earth with their spades, searching it deep with their cruel implements. With an endless repetition throughout the long scorching day, they lifted their arms and bent their bare yellow backs, down which the sweat ran in rivulets. The piercing rays of the sun tortured the naked parched land. It roasted to a darker brown the brown bodies of the Javanese coolies, and it burnt the white skins of the Europeans to a dull red hue. But from these uniformly yellow bodies it seemed to glide off powerless, as though they had been animated by a life more obstinate and ruthless than the gruelling heat that fell from the sky and rose again from the earth.

Along the edge of the forest, canals were being dug. There the Javanese coolies stood up to their thighs in the grey, putrid, evil-smelling water of the swamp. To each the mandur had allotted a task. Ruki looked straight ahead of him along the bed of the waterway which, almost choked with mud and vegetation, ran into the forest. Trees had fallen into it and across it, and lay there, together with decaying plants and dead animals, rotting into a black, slimy paste from which new plants were already shooting up vigorously. The water weeds and the scum formed a mass so dense that one would have placed one's foot confidently on top of it, to find with surprise that one suddenly sank away through it.

"Get on! Work!"

Ruki looked at his spade. It was new and shiny. Unwilling, loitering, Ruki pulled up his shorts still higher, and then stepped hesitatingly into the lukewarm, sticky water where millions of mosquito larvæ darted hither and thither just below the water weeds. He did not understand why this work had to be done. He could not realize all that had happened to him, and that he was no longer guarding his buffalo in the peaceful sunshine of the grasslands. He did not understand the power that had got him in its iron grip and compelled him . . . compelled him.

"Get on! Work!"

Again the 'mandur was shouting. The forest echoed his voice with a cavernous, ghostly sound that came back from the darkest depths. Ruki was startled and began to work, hacking deep into the mud with his spade. The mud gave way beneath his feet, and bubbles rose from between his widely-spread toes. Ahead of him and behind him other coolies worked. They stepped on with a glugging sound; their spades splashed into the water and were sucked down till they drew them up again with a burden that was thrown against the bank. These sounds were repeated endlessly. They formed a rhythm that was drowsy and soporific in the silence of the long drawn out day. Mechanically, as though asleep, they wielded their implements, lifted the mud, monotonously, again, again. . . . Sometimes they rested for a second. They spat into the palms of their hands, and with the backs of their hands wiped away the streams of perspiration that gushed from their foreheads into their eyes.

"Get on! Move on! Work!"

It was the voice of the mandur.

A louder voice followed: "Get on! Quicker! Quicker!" It was the assistant urging them to greater speed. He walked along the canal with big strides, his white suit fouled with mud. Obediently the coolies bent lower and continued to dig, casting furtive glances under their drooping eyelids at the tuan who was measuring and checking here and there the tasks allotted by the mandur. "Get on! Get on! Don't rest. Otherwise you will never finish your task!"

Why this hurry, wondered Ruki. If they didn't finish, well they didn't finish. Who could help it? Hadn't it always been like that? When he did not get home with the grass for his buffalo before sunset, sure enough he arrived after sunset, when it was dark. Had anybody ever said anything about it? It harmed no one. Who would be cutting the grass for the buffalo now? And what was nenneh doing? He ceased to be aware of his surroundings, the spade drooped in his hands, and he stared in front of him. He saw the campong, the grassy plain, Supinah. What was Karminah doing now? Would she also be standing in the mud, wet and sticky up to the hips? Or was she merely cooking for Marto? Where was Kromorejo? Where was Isah? And where, he wondered, were the maidens, where was the cheap gold? His ruminations were brutally interrupted by a blow in the face.

"Ough!" He was so startled that he let go of his spade. It fell down and disappeared beneath the murky water.

"Get on with your task! Why do you stand there dreaming, god damn you?"

Still reeling from the blow, and clumsily because he was afraid, he tried to find the spade. He hardly knew what he was doing. He only knew that close to him, towering above him, was the threatening figure of the tuan.

"Where is your spade, you buffalo? Find it at once!"

"Yes, sir."

Still more frightened because a European was addressing him directly, he sought for the spade awkwardly and ineffectually. The white man lost patience.

"What are you doing? You buffalo, you bastard! Do you know where your spade is? Or don't you?"

Ruki was so confused that he began to grin.

"Really . . . I don't know . . ." he stammered. He had not properly understood the assistant's question. His knowledge of Malay was very limited. In his terror he had only one idea: he must say in answer the things that the tuan wanted him to say.

But the European saw only the grin on the dark face. He sprang at Ruki and struck him with his open hand. "You monkey! You brute! Do you think you can be lazy here, and impertinent into the bargain? I'll teach you to laugh, by god! There!"

He stooped down, seized Ruki by his neck, and pushed his head under water. After a couple of seconds he allowed him to come up, and then pushed him under again. Meanwhile he scolded angrily in Dutch.

"You rotten novice! You good-for-nothing! I'll teach you, by god! Down into the mud, that's where you can laugh. Grin as much as you like now, you beastly black hound!"

Twice more he pushed Ruki down under water, a little longer each time. Stifled, frightened to death, he coughed out the mud from his nose and his mouth.

"Will you stop grinning now?"

"Yes, sir!"

"Will you work?"

"Yes, sir."

Tremblingly, Ruki answered "yes" to everything. If the assistant had told him at that moment to drive a knife into his own chest, he would still have answered "yes." In his terror he had only one desire: to avert this incomprehensible wrath, to escape this brute force. He stood there shaking and bowed down, not comprehending why all this was happening to him.

"Find your spade!"

"Yes, sir."

He bent down hastily, chanced upon the handle, pulled it above the water, and began to dig into the sucking, sticky mud. The water was running down from his hair, entering his eyes and his mouth. He swallowed several times because he did not dare spit out the dirty, stinking water in the presence of the tuan. For spitting before a person is the greatest insult imaginable, and Ruki was perfectly acquainted with the rules of native custom. The assistant continued to look at him for a few minutes. "If you haven't finished your task this afternoon, I'll give you another drubbing. Do you understand?"

"Yes, sir."

Without looking up, Ruki continued to labour. His back ached, the muscles of his arms shook with fatigue. He had to finish this afternoon. This afternoon, when was that? Was it sunset? Or earlier? He dared not rest. He dared not even pause for a second. All around him was the regular monotonous swish made by the others as they advanced slowly but steadily. The forest was full of sounds. A cicada sang its high penetrating tune. The sun rose higher, the heat increased. It burned the bent backs of the coolies. It was as though the heat and the vast silence had grown together into something so tense that it must burst. Slowly, hesitatingly, the seconds, each of them seeming infinite, passed.

One hour before midday the tension slackened at the call of the ton-tongs. Like a wave of sound, the noise rolled over the land, re-echoed from the forest, rose up to the empty, harshly glowing sky, and melted away into it. It was like a liberation. Suddenly the silence and the tension were broken. Work was interrupted, spades were thrown into a heap. The coolies were free to eat. Their voices rose over the wide plain, and from the distance the nasal sound of Chinese came back as in reply.

The tea arrived. Two contract coolies brought paraffin tins full of tea slung on rattan staves which they balanced over their shoulders. Each coolie took a drink of the warm, refreshing liquid from the coconut shell that hung by the side of each tin. From a banana leaf, they ate a portion of rice and a small piece of dried fish. Some of them bought their food from one of the so-called free women who cooked and sold food to the coolies without a woman of their own. They charged high prices, exploiting the men who had no time or opportunity to look after themselves. They grew rich at their trade, and carried their wealth about them in the form of English sovereigns sewn on to their jackets as ornaments.

After the meal, the coolies resumed their hard and tedious task. It went on till, just before dusk, the ton-tongs called them back to the compound. As they had gone to their work in the twilight before sunrise, so they returned from it in the twilight of evening. They walked in single file, spade on shoulder, too tired to mutter more than an occasional word. The black, sunburned skin of their bodies was covered with clots and streaks of mud Above their heads the sky turned from red to a leaden hue. The shadows, like some dark animal, crept towards them over the fields from the forest.

They bathed near the wells or in the river that flowed behind the compound. Some of them sharpened their spades or, if they had a child, fashioned a toy from an old cigarette tin and a piece of string. Others talked together or exchanged jokes with the women. Sometimes one of them tried to persuade a woman to spend a night with him in secret, promising her money or a sarong. Few of the men had a woman of their own, and the women from the campongs in the neighbourhood refused to have anything to do with the contract coolies—they were regarded as pariahs. These assignations meant the deception of the man to whom the woman had been allotted. It frequently led to fierce quarrels, and sometimes to murder. To the coolies, life was of little value, and murder for a woman's sake held no shame for them.

Ruki was crouching in front of his hut. He saw a woman coming back from the well. She wore nothing but a long cloth wrapped round her and tied over her breasts. On her head she carried a pile of wet clothes which she had been washing. Ruki looked at her. She was no longer young; she was much older than he. Her thin hair was hanging in a loose and untidy bun on her neck. Her hips were broad, and her breasts swung as she walked. She had a broad, flat nose, and her mouth was open.

"Isah!"

She stopped, and turned towards the man who had called her. "Yes?"

What a coarse voice she has, thought Ruki, startled for a moment to hear that she was Isah. He had been digging behind Kromorejo the whole day, and Kromorejo was no older than she. He saw other women coming from the well. Their bodies exhausted by work and child bearing, they most of them had a look of age. Only one here and there was young, elastic, desirable.

"Saïma! Saïma!"

A slender, very young Sundanese girl stood still. She had just been bathing. The garment she was wearing reached from her armpits to her knees. Her rounded smooth brown shoulders glistened with drops of water. Her blue-black hair hung loose and wet. Under the taut sarong, her firm young breasts stood up, quivering challengingly at every step. She walked, her hips slightly swaying, her belly slightly distended, a broad, fruitful womb.

"Saïma! Saïma!"

She stopped, just in front of Ruki, and lifted her head inquiringly to the manduress Minah, the fat, soldierly matron who had called her.

"Yes, mandur?"

"Mind you sharpen your spade!"

Saïma laughed. Her teeth shone white behind her red, made-up lips.

"Karmo is sharpening it for me, mandur."

"Slut!" said the manduress Minah, as she walked contemptuously past Saïma.

Saïma stood still a moment longer, watching with amusement Minah's corpulent, ridiculously dressed figure; she wore the clothes of a native woman with a European man's felt hat and black boots, the last being in Minah's opinion the most adequate symbols of her power.

Then Saïma's eyes met Ruki's covetous glance. She hid her face in the bend of her arm and giggled. Ruki jumped up, but a sudden confusion paralysed him. Saïma put down the pail of water she was carrying and lifted her arms in order to knot her hair. Her gesture pulled her sarong up above her knees. The beginnings of her sturdy, pale brown thighs were exposed. She held her body bent slightly backward. Her breasts trembled on her slender torso like over-ripe fruits. As she did up her hair, her handsome arms formed a frame round her small head, and again she laughed. In the hot flood that overwhelmed Ruki's thoughts and understanding, he no longer saw the soft round shape of her face, her glittering black eyes, her heavy brows, her nose which was no more than an outline, and her red mouth with its full lips. He saw only the swaying domes of her breasts, the white of her teeth, sharp as those of a carnivorous animal, and the gentle curve of her belly. Challengingly she caught his troubled glance, and asked: "Eh? Are you a newcomer? Where do you come from?"

Her voice was like the twittering of a bird. Ruki told her the name of his campong, and then bent down and picked up her pail. They crossed the compound square. On the other side, the first of a long row, was Saïma's hut. Ruki put down the pail.

"Who is your man?" he asked.

She giggled. "I follow Parman. He used to be mandur, but tuan is angry with him, and now he is a coolie again."

They were silent. They could hardly see each other in the fast gathering darkness. Then she asked: "On the night of pay-day. . . . Do you gamble then?"

"Yes," said Ruki proudly, "I gamble."

There was a silence, and then she asked: "And if you win, what do you do with the money?"

"I buy gold with it," said Ruki without hesitation. "Gold coins."

There was a further silence. A figure detached itself from the darkness. A man came towards them.

"That is Parman," said Saïma.

"What do you want here?" snarled Parman, an old, sturdy Javanese.

"Nothing, Pa. I carried Saïma's pail of water for her."

Parman pushed open the low wooden door. He lived alone with Saïma. He had behind him seven years of contract labour, and it was only this year that a woman had been allotted to him. She was handsome and young, it is true, but she gave herself to any man who would pay her, and now she had begun to go to the Chinese, who paid more; and she never gave him any of the money she earned in this way, but bought silken jackets and kaïns and sometimes even gold. It made no difference if he beat her. She merely screamed and raved like one possessed. She was a wicked woman, and he was no longer young; but all the same she belonged to him, and he did not like to be made ridiculous before the other men of the compound. Of course, they too were deceived, but not so openly, not so shamelessly. Saïma was a born hussy. Three times already a man had been knifed on her account. Two of them had died. And he himself had lost his position as mandur owing to her.

Saïma stooped down and picked up the pail.

"Food will be ready in a minute," she shouted and, passing close to Ruki, she whispered quickly: "If you win, I'm willing."

Then she disappeared with the pail into the hut. The door fell to behind her, and Ruki sought his own room on the other side of the dark compound square. He was on his couch before the ton-tong sounded. He was tired. His body ached. As on the previous night, he lay with his knees drawn up and one of his hands under his head. His ear glowed against the palm of his hand. He did not hear his companions come in. He did not hear the mosquitoes buzzing round his ears. Nor did he notice the squeaking, noisy love making of the rats.

Late in the night he woke up and looked round. By the glimmer of the oil lamp, he could vaguely see Kromorejo's couch: once again he was not alone. . . . Restlessly Ruki turned on his other side.

## vi

IN front of the assistant's house in section one sat the coolies in long rows. They were waiting to be paid. Karminah, her head bowed slightly, her eyes cast down, glanced sideways from beneath her eyelids.

"When they call you, you must stand up and say 'yes,' " whispered the woman who was squatting by her side. She was feeding a child at the breast. Karminah nodded, and looked down at the small shaved head, at the brown, wrinkled breast.

"And then," the woman went on in a whisper, "you go to the little table."

"Silence!" thundered the assistant. For a moment, there was dead silence. Their downcast eyelids and pinched mouths seemed to express the utmost indifference: they gave not the slightest indication of the passions that were within them. Only the tinkle of silver coins, the low murmur of the clerk, and an occasional sharp word from the assistant could be heard.

"Then you go to the tuan's little table," continued the woman, "and then . . ."

"Silence! Damn it all! Who is it who dares to open his mouth here?" shouted the assistant in a fury as he glanced searchingly down the ranks. "Always those women! Can't the hussies learn to keep their mouths shut? Mandur Sumo, go and stand by the women."

Mandur Sumo, a delicately made Javanese, went and stood by the side of the manduress who was in charge of the women.

"Silence!" he said in a feeble attempt to display his power. But there was no conviction in his voice, and the hasty glance which he cast now and then at the assistant spoke of the same utter indifference as the closed faces of the coolies.

A child began to whimper and suddenly cried aloud. "Sh! sh!" murmured its frightened mother. A woman by her side took the child, opened her jacket, and gave it her breast. Perfectly satisfied, the child began to suck at the new breast.

Rapidly, in a voice of command and with monotonous regularity, the assistant called out the names of the coolies. Humbly, bending low, they came up to the little table, and took the money due to them. They never looked at how much there was, and had not the slightest idea of the sum to which they were entitled. Silent and self-effacing, they left the courtyard of the assistant's house and walked back to the compound, where the Malay pedlars were already gathering with their sweetmeats, their jackets and kaïns, their gaming-mats.

"Rukinah!"

"Yes." Hurriedly the woman by Karminah's side stood up.

"Three guilders and thirty-seven cents."

As she raked the money from the table, she dropped a few cents, and shouted with a hysterical giggle: "Eh, I've dropped it! I've dropped it!" There was suppressed laughter among the other women.

The assistant shook his head. "Those women! Always at sea!"

Rukinah laughed, hiding her mouth in a corner of her slendang. The child looked up with great wise velvety eyes at the tuan.

"Women . . ." lisped the Javanese mandur with aristocratic contempt.

"Karminah!"

There was no response.

"Karminah!"

A woman nudged her. "Hey, quickly! You!"

"Yes," said Karminah, startled.

The women were giggling again. She stood in front of the table awkwardly, not knowing how to behave. The assistant's eyes rested on her for a moment. She looked clean and tidy in her light-coloured, carefully folded sarong. Round her slim waist she wore a broad, many-coloured scarf. The lines of her little rounded shoulders and her small girlish breasts showed through her fresh-looking, flowered jacket. In her heavy knot of hair was a fiery red flower. She stood there with downcast eyes, and the vein in the hollow of her neck beat fast with nervousness. She placed her small hands together so that only the pointed tips of her fingers touched each other.

"You are one of the new coolies, aren't you?"

She was so frightened that she caught her breath. "Yes, tuan," she brought out at last.

"What did you do when you were in Java?"

A pause. "I was babu, tuan, with a Dutch mevrouw, tuan."

"Oh, were you? Ahem! . . . Who is your man?"

The women nudged each other secretly and giggled.

"Silence, you there!" The voice of the assistant thundered over them. They stifled all sounds; they almost ceased to breathe.

"Who is your man?"

"I follow Marto, tuan."

"Oh. . . . Here are your wages, one guilder forty-three cents."

"Many thanks, tuan."

She picked up the money in her delicate hand with its red-painted nails. For a moment the assistant followed her with his eyes, a small figure walking through his garden, a tiny precious doll with the gait of a queen.

The monotonous roll-call continued till the last woman had been paid. After the Javanese came the Chinese. Then the assistant quickly settled with the mandurs and the under-mandurs, and gave orders about the work to be done after hari besar.

Darkness fell rapidly, creeping over the plain, and climbing up the hillock on which the house stood. It swallowed up the house. From the distant compound came the subdued sound of a melody played on the gamelan. The hens clucked on the perches in the still open chicken house. The assistant rose from the table and ordered the furniture to be taken in. As the boy hurried forward to do his bidding, the mandurs prepared to leave.

"Tabeh, tuan. Tabeh, tuan."

"Tabeh," he said, returning their greeting carelessly. He was plunged in thought. Then, suddenly looking up, he said: "Oh . . . er . . . mandur Muïn. . . ."

"Yes, tuan?"

The other mandurs went their way discreetly. They felt at once that the tuan wanted to discuss a confidential matter.

"Marto . . . is he Karminah's man?"

"Yes, tuan. Marto is an old coolie. He has been begging for a woman for a long time."

"Hm . . . yes."

The mandur waited discreetly, hat in hand.

"Hm . . . yes. Send the woman here to-night."

There was a silence.

"As tuan desires. But . . ." said Muïn hesitatingly.

"Well?"

"Marto was promised a woman a long time ago, and nobody knows yet when a new batch of contract hands will arrive."

"Send them both to me."

"Yes, tuan. Tabeh, tuan."

"Tabeh, Muïn."

The last figure slipped away into the dark. Muïn went straight to Marto's hut.

"Where is Karminah?"

"She is cooking, mandur. Why? Is anything wrong?"

"You and she are to go together to the tuan's house."

"Why, mandur?"

"The tuan wants your woman."

Marto looked at the mandur in silence. He was an old Javanese, lean and ill-cared for.

"But I have waited so long for a woman," he brought out at last.

"Can I help that? The tuan wants her. Presently, when more women come, you'll be given one. Do you understand?"

"Yes, mandur."

Karminah listened in frightened silence.

"Why must I go to the tuan?" she asked.

Marto looked at her and shook his head. Women, he thought, they are stupider than buffaloes. Then he answered: "But because you please the tuan, of course."

Hesitatingly she remained standing, brooding over the strange things that were happening to her.

"Hurry up! Go and wash, or else your hands will smell of fish. Perhaps you'll become the tuan's housekeeper, and then you won't have to dig any more."

Without realizing it, Karminah lifted up her hands. Inside they were blistered and sore. She had never before done work of the kind she was compelled to do now. She smiled.

"May I eat first?" she asked.

"Yes, but quickly."

"Yes."

* * * * *

Dunk was sitting on his dimly lit veranda. It had been dry for a long time, and there were few mosquitoes. He pored over his newspaper, trying to decipher the letters, but his thoughts kept wandering. A month ago he had had to send away his housekeeper. She was with child, and he did not want children. He had warned her of the consequences of pregnancy when she had come to him four years before. For four years everything had gone perfectly, and then suddenly . . .

She had asked if she might go to a midwife in the town. He had made no objection. When she was well again, she could come back. She cooked very well, looked after his clothes and other possessions, and kept him informed of all that happened in the compound and of the talk that went on there. He had grown used to her; but children by her . . . no. That he would not have.

Now that she had gone, he found that he missed her. The household did not go on in its usual way. Besides, he needed her as a woman. . . . What an attractive little girl that Karminah was! What a fragile figure! How much he had learned to like them, these slender, supple, brown women. Sometimes he compared them with the European women he had met when on leave. How much he preferred the women here! And they were so much more submissive, so much more adaptable, so much more womanly.

Din, the house-boy, came in on tiptoe.

"Tuan!"

"Yes?"

"Marto and his woman are here."

"Right. Send them to the front of the house."

"Yes, tuan."

A moment later there was a gentle sound of steps in the dark courtyard, then a cough. Dunk looked up, and went to the top of the steps.

"Marto?"

"Yes, tuan."

"Marto, your woman is called Karminah, isn't she?"

"Yes. Karminah, tuan."

"Here are ten guilders for you." Dunk handed the coolie a bank-note. The coolie accepted it with polite thanks.

"Tell Karminah to wait near the kitchen till I call her. As soon as the new coolies arrive, you shall have first choice among the women. I will see to it myself."

"As tuan wishes. Tabeh, tuan."

"Tabeh, Marto."

Dunk could hear them walking back to the annexes through the darkness. During the transaction that had changed her owner, the woman had not uttered a word. Now he caught the sound of her voice asking a question softly, and of the man's short, murmured reply. He could also hear conversation going on behind the out-buildings. He knew that Karminah was sitting there waiting until he called her.

He continued to stare outside across the balustrade. It was a still, moonlit night. Faint, diaphanous clouds drifted past the narrow sickle of the moon and across the deep blue sky. The stars twinkled and flickered like red and blue and violet sparks. The land lay under the lofty dome of the sky, flat and dark, with the virgin forest rising from it in the distance. Over everything lay an impressive, peaceful quietude—a quietude only accentuated by the heavy rhythm of the gamelan.

The night was sublime and serene, too majestic almost for love—for love of the body, at any rate. Or perhaps it was just for this kind of love, which is the same in all forms of life, that such a night had been made. Was it not perhaps the lowly love of the flesh that was alone possible in the midst of all this glory? A purely spiritual ecstasy would have seemed ridiculously inadequate against the background of this divine, silver-blue mystery.

Through Dunk's mind passed no such clear thoughts; but he felt a kind of vague relationship between his physical desire and the devout music of the gamelan, the stillness of the tropic night. If he had consciously meditated on the question at all, he would probably have explained this relationship in his realistic formula: "Rather an Eastern woman than a Western."

He stretched himself suddenly, almost voluptuously, till he felt all his muscles grow taut. Then he relaxed again, and called the boy.

"Tuan?"

From the dark recesses of the out-buildings rose the reply above the subdued murmurs of the servants. Hurriedly, with his coat only half on, the boy stood a moment later before Dunk.

"Gin and bitters!"

"Yes, tuan."

The boy disappeared and came back a moment later carrying a tray which he placed before Dunk, who poured himself out a drink. In one gulp he emptied the glass, then he smacked his lips, and sat with the glass in his hand, meditatively considering the progress of the warming stream from his mouth to his stomach. He filled the glass again, lit a cigarette, and fished up the paper which he had dropped on the floor.

The silence around him was unbroken. Now and then a mosquito buzzed past his ear. Then he glanced up; but he observed nothing of his surroundings, so accustomed was he to the mellowed intimacy of the old rattan furniture, the white crochet cover over the table, the maidenhair ferns on the tall, characterless stands, the dingy curtain with discoloured flower border that hung at the entrance to the dining-room, the faded prints in gilded frames and the large painted plate which he had once brought home from a sale at the end of a wild night. By the side of the entrance near the outside steps stood a rickety rattan hat-stand loaded with sun helmets long since superannuated, but faithfully preserved by Louki, his former housekeeper, together with a stained felt hat that dated from his last leave. Suspended from the wall were two thick rattan walking sticks and a whip.

In every assistant's house he had inherited, the veranda had looked exactly the same. When he arrived in Deli eleven years ago, he had arranged the first house he had had like that, and ever since, after each removal, the new veranda had been arranged with the same furniture in the same places, faithfully placed according to the customary plan by Louki and the boy. The hats, the sticks, and the whip hung in harmony. Dunk liked it to be arranged in that way, for then he knew the position of everything by touch, and it meant that he was at once at home in each new house.

At last he folded up his newspaper, stretched once more, emptied his glass, and stood up to go to his bath. Silently he splashed water over himself, and over the floor of the bathroom. Again and again he dipped water from the large Chinese porcelain tank and poured it over himself, hurrying as though to enjoy the cooling of his body as long as possible; but no sooner had he dried himself than he felt once more the warm, clammy air sticking to his body. When he had put on his sarong, he called the boy.

"Serve dinner, and tell the woman to come in."

"Yes, tuan."

He lingered a little and continued to walk round the room, hanging the towel over a chair and rearranging the bottles on his toilet table. Meanwhile he listened to the murmur of voices in the outbuildings and heard Din's voice saying loudly and without ceremony: "Get up! Tuan is asking for you."

Did he perceive a subdued chuckle? Was it the water carrier and his wife? Suddenly, he was annoyed at the absolute lack of discretion in the whole situation. The European in him rebelled against the Oriental unreserve in matters of sex relationships.

But then his attention was attracted by hesitating footsteps near his door. They were light steps that moved on the lazy atmosphere like the sigh of the wind. They were followed by the noisier steps of Din, a little hurried, rattling his serving tray full of plates and glasses. Then he heard Din's voice, half encouraging and half irritated. "Now then, step inside. Hurry up! Tuan is waiting for you."

Dunk himself opened the door and stood face to face with the slight, stooping figure of a woman. She crept past him like a shadow and squatted down inside the room.

"Oh," said Dunk with a smile, trying to be as natural as possible. Almost at once her shyness made him feel quietly superior. "You have arrived? You may stand up."

"Yes, tuan. Tabeh, tuan."

Her voice scarcely rose above the silence. She rose to her feet, and fidgeted at her slendang where it covered her small breasts. From below the sarong her small brown feet looked out like two frightened birds. Dunk felt almost sorry for her. It awoke within him a desire to protect her, to win this childishly subtle girl-woman for himself. He wanted to make those large, startled dark eyes look at him with confidence.

"Are you frightened?" He had placed himself in front of her.

"No, tuan."

How inexpressibly fragile she seemed by the side of his sturdy Teutonic strength. He lifted the slendang from her shoulders. She shuddered at his touch. Smiling, with his hand still on her arm, he teased her.

"I believe you're frightened all the same."

"No, tuan, I am not frightened." The low voice was deeply serious. He bent his head towards her, and for one second touched her cool smooth skin. But he drew back at once. Coconut oil, he thought, with a momentary disappointment. He had cured Louki of the habit of putting coconut oil on her hair long since.

Karminah, on the other hand, drew back from his breath instinctively because it had a sharp smell of gin. Never before had she smelt alcohol, and with a sideways glance she looked at his white skin which was spotted red from prickly heat. She had known hitherto only dark skins that were cool and smooth as the leaf of a banana. He recovered first, and pointed to the bathroom.

"There is the bathroom, you see, Karminah? And here is a towel. Now you must bathe, and also wash your hair very carefully. Will you? You must use soap."

"Yes, tuan."

He led her to the washstand with a gentle but compelling hand.

"And then, when your hair is a little dry, you may put on it something from one of these bottles. Do you smell?" He held an open bottle with some lotion before her nose. "You can use this, or something else. There are quite a lot of bottles, you see? And now you may choose for yourself the one you think the nicest of the lot." He tried to speak a little lightly, and to establish some kind of intimacy. But she remained solemn, obedient. Round the small mouth there was no trace of a smile.

"Yes, tuan." For a moment she had looked up with astonishment at all the things standing on the little shelf over the washstand.

"Have you eaten, Karminah?"

"Yes, tuan."

"Good. Well, I'm going to eat now. Meanwhile, have your bath, and wait for me till I come back."

"Yes, tuan."

She was left by herself. First she remained for some time in the same spot without moving. Then she lifted her face and looked at her own eyes in the mirror. Next she peered carefully round. She ventured to take a step towards the bed, opened the mosquito net, passed her hand over the sheet, and felt the pillow. This, at any rate, was not new. It was a bed just like that of the njonja she had served in Java. But . . . would she sleep there now? With the tuan? She lowered her head and hid her face in her arms to smother the giggles that suddenly burst out at this thought. Hastily she slipped away from the bed, and after some further hesitation she took the towel and crept down the wooden steps towards the bathroom.

Her long wet hair still loose over her back, she came up again. She had dressed again entirely. There she stood in front of the washstand. Her thin little fingers roamed among the bottles and the flasks. She wondered whatever there could be in all these bottles. She had been a babu for a short time only and hardly knew anything of the habits of Europeans. Like an inquisitive child, she fumbled among the corks and the glass stoppers, forgetting why she was there, forgetting also the man who was in the next room and would hold her in his arms before long. She shook the bottles and smelt them without knowing what to choose. Sometimes she poured a few drops into the palm of her hand, smelt at them and sniffed up the perfume.

"Boy!"

"Tuan!"

She started from her play and looked anxiously towards the door from behind which came the noise of a chair being moved aside. The blood suddenly rushed through her veins. Would he come in now? Was she frightened? Allah-il-allah! Yes, she was frightened. Frightened to death, and she felt ashamed also. She felt extremely ashamed. She thought of the act of love. How would it be with a white man, with such an utter stranger? She remembered the smell of alcohol on his breath, and the odour of his body that was damp, of another race. It was like the smell of a corpse, she thought suddenly. And then she thought of the rash on his skin, and then with beating heart she thought of the order he had given her.

She was to put on her hair what she liked best so that it should be perfumed. It was to be perfumed for him. And following the deepest instinct of the Moslem woman who blindly obeys the will of the man, she felt quickly along the shelf, hesitating still as to what would really be the best, and what, in her opinion, would please him most. Then, while she heard his steps shaking the house, she resolutely put out her little hand and unscrewed the top of the bottle of Odol. She felt it sting the skin under her hair. It hurt her. It brought the tears into her eyes. Trembling in every limb, she squatted down in the farthest corner of the room. She heard him come in. With downcast eyes, her little brown face a smooth impenetrable mask and her delicate hands clasped and shaking, she waited for what was to come. She knew nothing more. The room had faded from her consciousness, and she knew nothing more except that the tall white man was there who was about to possess her.

## VII

IT was the night of pay-day. With seven other coolies Ruki sat before the gambling mat. They played in silence, their eyes riveted as by a magnet to the inverted half coconut shell under which the little top was spinning. They listened intensely to the thin sound that came from under the brown polished shell. Then, when at last the little top ceased to revolve and dropped dead on the plate, they said: "Ng. . . ."

The tension grew tenser still, but their excitement was noticeable only from the fact that they sat up a little straighter and made an almost imperceptible movement with their delicate fingers. One of the players very carefully lifted up the shell. He did it very slowly, with an almost superstitous disinclination to hasten the fatal moment. He bent down slowly towards the little plate, looking underneath the half raised shell. Then, suddenly, with a gesture he came to life again, exclaiming: "Ts . . . wah . . . klabang!" The other gamblers, as though they had wakened from a spell, also lost their rigidity, bent over the little top, and sat up again.

"Ts . . . ts . . . ts . . wah . . . klabang!"

Those who had put their money on the little mat upon the section of klabang—the centipede—took up their winnings. They were self-possessed now and apparently passionless. Those who had lost grinned as they watched the winners take up the coins and arrange them in little heaps before them.

Stakes were placed again. Ruki ventured but one cent at a time. He had scarcely anything left of his wages. The unboiled rice ration given to him by the tuan had been taken away from him by Kromorejo. He had tried to resist, but Kromorejo was the stronger, and had, besides, become a contract coolie long before Ruki. A newcomer like Ruki had no rights even in the compound. He had gone hungry for days. At first one of the older coolies sometimes gave him something to eat. Then he arranged to have meals from one of the free women. By this arrangement he had enough to eat, but it absorbed practically the whole of his wages, so that only a few cents were left over for gambling. He had no clothes except the shorts, now dirty and threadbare, and the jacket in which he had come from Java—the manduress Minah had taken his kaïn.

The stakes had been placed. Ruki had put his on the frog. Beyond the mat and its primitive pictures Ruki saw the laughing mouth of Saïma. He watched in silence as one of the gamblers spun the little top on the plate. Spellbound, they riveted their eyes once more to the top, which was covered with a gesture that was reverent, mystic, superstitious. Again they sat motionless round the inverted coconut shell in the fantastic light thrown into the encircling darkness by the few oil lamps. The eight silent men were rigid as statues, their faces devoid of the slightest trace of expression, their hands folded in their laps, their legs crossed under them. Only their eyes lived. Deep in their pupils there seemed to burn a fire of madness. The little top fell down with a rattle. The cover was lifted very carefully.

"Wah . . . . klabang!"

The centipede again. It was as though Satan were taking part in the game. Four times running the centipede had appeared. Their voices rose and they all laughed loud and bitterly because they had been caught. Ruki alone maintained his seriousness. With downcast head, he stared sternly in front of him. Then he counted his money. Thirteen cents remained in the moist palm of his hand. He must win. He looked enviously at his neighbour who had won and continued to win on the klabang. Silver coins glimmered white among the dull bronze money. He noticed nothing else. He did not see the Malay fruit and vegetable sellers who sat in long rows in the compound square with their wares exhibited before them on little mats. On each mat a small oil lamp stood smoking. Every now and then the face of the vendor came within the vague ruddy circle of light which it threw. Most of them had worn-out, furrowed faces, old before their time—the faces of sickly folk emaciated by malaria and other diseases of the blood. Many of the women carried a child at their loose sagging breasts. Bigger children sat by their parents or, rolled in a kaïn, slept in the midst of the medley of people, baskets, and bales that littered the ground. Dogs in search of something to eat sniffed about. Laughter and shouts rose from the dark masses of brown humanity, but they were rarely noisy or exuberant. Over everything dripped the melancholy, resigned notes of the gamelan in a seemingly eternal repetition of the same motif; and high above stood the dark blue arch of the sky with its silent, burning constellations.

Deaf, blind, senseless to everything else, Ruki continued to play, losing one cent after the other. Then he pulled off his jacket and staked that. Again he lost. He sat on a little longer, following the game with bitter envy towards those who could still continue. Then, without a word, he rose from among them.

"Aren't you playing any more?"

"No."

But already they had ceased to pay any attention to him; the top had been spun again.

Through the whimsical play of light and shadow Ruki sought a way to his little hut, making himself a passage through the throng. From time to time he stopped at the stall of a free woman selling sweetmeats. His eyes rested longingly on all the pastries and the red and green drinks in coarse glasses. He was hungry; but he had not even any tobacco left. He went on, ill-tempered and depressed, and stopped for a moment to watch one of the other gambling mats. As he turned away to continue his walk he stumbled over a long figure wrapped in a dark kaïn that lay on the ground.

"Ts . . ." he exclaimed, annoyed because the others were laughing at him. "What is it? Eh? Who is it?"

One of the gamblers glanced hastily at the recumbent figure. "It is Karmin. He is ill."

Ruki lingered a moment. There had been something in the feel of that body that compelled his attention. He bent over it and struck a match.

"But he is dead!" he said.

The gamblers lifted their heads with an air of incredulity. Ruki pulled the dead man's kaïn on one side so as to see the face, and struck another match. The dancing flame suddenly lit up the olive green, contracted face. In the midst of the darkness the extinguished eyes stared at the trembling light. Round the mouth lines of pain were drawn. One of the hands was pressed violently against the chin. The little flame danced up for a moment, passing over the piteous death mask. Then suddenly it went out, and there remained nothing but a dark figure, an obscure and indefinite obstacle on the dark square.

"Ts . . . ts . . . ts!" exclaimed the gamblers, childishly astonished. "Ts . . . ts . . . eh! He is dead."

Then they turned towards the little top that had finished spinning and lay silent on the white plate. The cover was lifted very slowly and very carefully. Their eyes followed every movement of the man who performed the rite. They bent forward: it was kodok —the frog.

"Kodok!"

"Eh! . . . kodok!"

Their voices rose, they laughed as they pronounced the word. Then there was silence again, as they carefully put their money down on one of the squares of the mat or on one of the points where four squares met. They gambled on till the day broke, and when the daylight came again the corpse was still lying by their side.

As he reached the hut, Ruki bent down to the tin of water that stood under the porch. He was thirsty.

"Ruki!" It was the whispering voice of a woman that called. Without drinking, he stood up and listened keenly.

"Ruki!"

"Saïma?"

She giggled. Ruki pushed the little door open. Inside a small lamp was burning. It threw a little light in front of the hut, and in its glimmer he could see her there.

"What do you want?" he asked angrily in order to hide his shame at having lost.

"Nothing," she said, and giggled again.

"Go away," he said, "go to your man, or are you on your way to the Chinese again?"

"The Chinese pay well," she said.

"Aren't you ashamed, you a Sundanese woman, to go with Chinese who eat pig's meat?"

"But am I not orang kontrak? So why shouldn't I go with the Chinese? We are not in Java here. Everything is different."

"Chinese harlot!" said Ruki contemptuously.

The insult infuriated her. "Well, and why not? What does it matter? The Chinese are better men by far than you. Do you realize that? They treat us more considerately. They love a woman, and they pay. They pay in gold. But you, contract dogs, what do you pay? A quarter of a guilder, half a guilder perhaps."

"I pay well," said Ruki. Saïma's jacket had opened while she gesticulated, and he could see her hard firm breasts. Now he was thinking only of her body. She looked at him with distrust.

"Pay? What will you pay? New hands never have money."

"But I have money. I have been gambling. I have won. If you are willing, I can give you gold too, a small English coin. Gold!"

The magic word hung in the darkness. She breathed heavily.

"If you give that . . . gold . . ." Suddenly she placed herself in front of him. A heavy penetrating perfume of jasmine rose from her hair. He placed his hand on her shoulder. Through her thin clothes he felt her cool, resilient flesh. In utter silence they stood there in the darkness, not speaking to one another. Through the jasmine rose the heavy odour of her body, and suddenly his heart began to beat irregularly as though too much blood were coursing through it.

"Go inside!" he said briefly. It was like an order. He entered the hut first. She followed him. He pushed her down upon his couch and had no other knowledge than the warmth of her supple body against his, of her skin that was cool and yet flaming, and, losing himself in his primitive blind passion, he knew no more. . . . He did not know that she embodied all his dreams. Supinah also, and Karminah.

She folded her sarong neatly about her again so that the stiff edge of the right side fell down her left leg. Then she wound the violent pink silk scarf round her tiny waist and re-knotted her hair. She did it in one movement, holding the long silver hairpin with its flat ornamented head in her mouth meanwhile. Then she took the pin from between her lips and pushed it through the heavy bun.

"Where is the gold?"

Ruki leaned nonchalantly against the doorpost.

"What gold?"

"The gold you promised to give me."

"Give you gold? But how can I give you gold? I haven't a cent in the world." He laughed shortly, and turned his back to her. For a moment Saïma was silent. Here was a thought that her brain could not grasp at once. Then she realized that Ruki had cheated her. She awoke like a fury from her hard thinking. Her voice was furious as she shrieked hysterically.

"You dirty contract hound! So you want women without paying for them, do you? You've a right to talk about the Chinese, haven't you, you pig, you monkey, you bastard?"

"Silence!" said Ruki.

"Silence? Silence, indeed! A moment ago you didn't say silence, did you, when you wanted me? Then you had plenty to say for yourself, you dirty crocodile. Go to the devil! Yes, go to the devil!"

Her voice was loud and shrill, and sounded right across the compound square. Wirio, Sentono's woman, came out of the hut next door. She looked on foolishly, her mouth wide open. Other people began to gather round the doorway where Saïma stood scolding.

"Off with you!" said Ruki.

"Off with me! Off with me! I can go now, can I? A moment ago I was to stay, wasn't I? You liar. Yes, you're a greater teller of tales. That's all you can do! Yes, lying and womanising, and nothing else."

"What are you shouting about like this?" asked the manduress Minah in a threatening voice.

"Why am I shouting?" yelled Saïma pointing at Ruki. "Why? Because this crocodile promises me gold, and hasn't got a cent in the world."

The onlookers grinned. They thought it great fun to see somebody else cheated. They considered it clever to cheat. But their laughter made Saïma's fury flare up with even greater violence.

"First he gambles and loses. And then he wants a woman. The cheat! The liar!"

"Do go away," muttered Ruki in a toneless voice.

"Away!" she shouted ironically, without a trace of shame before the large crowd of people who had gathered. She put her hands on her hips and, arms akimbo, stood there challenging him with her beautiful body. "Now I'm to go away! Less than an hour ago you did not mind if I stayed, did you?"

Now the laughter of the onlookers was at Ruki's expense. They felt that Saïma by her invective had got the better of him. He was still leaning against the doorpost, staring straight before him, as though the hot stream of reproaches slid off his back without affecting him. Saïma continued to shout and to shriek, working herself up into an hysterical rage.

Then, slightly lifting his head, Ruki said, scarcely moving his lips: "Oh dear! The Chinese harlot! She has eaten pig's meat with the Chinese, and now the devil has entered her."

The jeers and laughter rose again, almost smothering Saïma's enraged protests.

"Yes," she said, "I have eaten pig's meat, and why not? And I do sleep with men who eat pig's meat! What about the other contract women? What about the women who sleep with the white men, with the tuans? Well, what about them? Your wife, Karminah, she is a housekeeper now in section one. Is that in accordance with the old customs of Java? Isn't she living with a kafir, an unbeliever?"

The manduress Minah considered it was time for her to interfere. Broad and strong, her matronly body towered over Saïma's slender figure.

"Stop it! Be quiet! Enough of this! You need not insult the tuans."

"Silence? I shan't be quiet. I don't hold my tongue for a man, and I certainly won't for a woman."

Saïma was shouting at the top of her voice. The manduress Minah looked at her. Into her broad bulging face came a harsh expression. Her protruding eyes and her wide mouth grew threatening, and she looked more than ever like a frog. She spat out a broad stream of betel juice. It gave an orange red tinge to her dark lips. She planted her broad feet with their widespread toes solidly into the sandy soil —boots she wore only when at work. Then she pulled up one of her sleeves.

"Now then, you creature! Along with you to your husband! Aren't you ashamed to humiliate him before all the other men?"

"I am ashamed of nothing," yelled Saïma. "Were they ashamed when they gave me as a present to a man, just as you would give someone a dog? That's how they gave me away. Parman is not my hsuband. I follow him only because I am made to. I follow him because my name is orang kontrak, and I don't care a bit. Let him feel ashamed! And I don't care if I am a Chinese harlot. If I feel like it, I'll go again to their camp. Where do you think I earn my gold? Not with the spade, do you?"

"And now that's enough! Silence! At once!" The manduress Minah came and stood immediately in front of Saïma; but once more Saïma's shrieking voice replied: "Ah! you can give orders when we're at work. Now it isn't work time!"

With a grab, more sudden than one would have thought possible from such a heavy woman, the manduress Minah seized Saïma by the hair. She pulled and tugged at the heavy knot. The pin dropped out of it, and all the hair unrolled. The long black tresses gave Minah a firm hold. She pulled Saïma's head down, pushed her on to the ground, and pressed her face into the sand. At first Saïma underwent the ill-usage without uttering a sound. Her obstinate silence infuriated the mandaress. She struck the prone woman with increasing violence, dragged at her hair, slapped her face, and all the while she shouted abusive names at her in a hotter and hotter rage.

She pinched and scratched Saïma, and rubbed her face over the sand. She was no longer meting out punishment: she was giving vent to blind hysterical rage, to uncontrolled personal hatred. Her thwarted desire for domination exerted itself with the more fury because the victim made no complaint.

But at last Saïma gave in.

"Have pity, manduress! Pity!"

"No, you child of sin! Silence! Silence!"

Saïma was howling now. But still she refused to beg her tormentor's pardon. She continued to shout only: "Pity! Pity! Pity!" Then she burst into frenzied cries, yelling continually as loud as she could. New spectators arrived from all over the compound, and asked in whispers what was happening.

"The manduress Minah is beating Saïma," the others replied, and this seemed a completely satisfactory answer to the newcomers. At last, when a broad stream of blood began to flow from her forehead, Saïma said: "I beg your pardon!" But she said it as she had said the other things, shrieking, yelling, howling: "Pardon! Pardon! Pardon!"

Minah, who was out of breath, stopped at once.

She re-arranged her own hair. Lying at her feet, Saïma continued to howl: "Pity! Pardon!"

"Silence!"

Her head on the ground, Saima went on howling. She shook violently with convulsive sobs.

"Silence!"

Saima ceased to make a sound. She sat up and began to look round her with the dazed look of one who comes out of a trance. Her hair hung loose around her, and her jacket was torn to tatters. Her face was covered with blood and dirt. One of her eyes was swollen. From time to time she felt it carefully, but absent-mindedly, automatically.

"Get along!"

Obediently she rose and walked in silence through the spectators and across the compound square towards her hut, where Parman squatted smoking.

"Did the manduress Minah beat you?" he asked.

She made no reply. She took a piece of broken comb from a ledge and began to tidy her hair. From time to time Parman glanced at her over his shoulder, and in the flicker of the oil lamp he perceived that her face was swollen and disfigured.

"That's what you get for your impertinence."

She said nothing in reply. She did not even look at him. She dipped a corner of her torn jacket into a tin of water and dabbed her wound and her eyelid. Then she lay down on the couch and fell asleep.

The coolies dispersed from before Ruki's hut. Here and there a laugh resounded as they discussed the event. It had diverted them enormously. They loitered on and returned to the gaming mats or to the stalls of the free women where they continued to converse.

Ruki squatted down. He stared across the compound square at the tenuous shadows that fluttered in all directions. The sound of the gamelan reached him, monotonous, peaceful, dreamy, pious. The very first breeze of early morning rustled the leaves of the coconut palms.

Close to Ruki a figure bent down and picked something up from the ground. It was Kromorejo: he had found Saïma's silver hairpin. He slipped it into his pocket. It could be sold to a Chinese.

# PART II

I

THE days came and the days went. They grew together into an endlessly long chain of equal shanks never varying in size or in colour. Fourteen days' work, one day's rest. Fourteen days of slavery, toil, drudgery. One day of gambling, smoking, and squatting in conversation about infinitesimal events. The ton-tong signalled the coolies to rise. The ton-tong signalled them to bed. The monotonous routine stifled all desire to object or resist. They worked mechanically without thinking, without even knowing why. They knew nothing of markets, of trade, of the speculation that went on in the white world.

Ruki performed his task with patience. His brown feet sank into the brown earth, his brown body was one with the brown soil into which he drove his spade.

The sun poured down its molten glow pitilessly, and the air trembled under its singeing rays. There was a threat of rain. Clouds began to pile up and expand into gigantic shapes which put themselves between sun and earth. Then their all-pervading shadow covered the young rubber trees, the patient brown hands, the glistening yellow backs. Everything was steeped in unearthly silence. Tremendous events seemed to be preparing. Nature lay panting and paralysed under the blinding glow that fell from the sky in yellow, brassy streaks. The wind had died away. On the horizon stood the tropical forest stock-still. The leaves of the heveas hung down flabby and motionless. Oppressed by the growing heat, the coolies performed their task in silence, now and then wiping away, with a gesture that had become habitual, the drops of sweat that oozed from their faces.

Ruki glanced up at the sky. Large white clouds were piling up, towering into Titanic piles that rose threateningly above the flat world. Livid patches appeared among the cloudy monsters, which turned leaden in colour and then almost black. Their desolate, dead colour communicated itself to the earth. Everything became toneless and vague. Still the silence and the heat increased ominously. Yet behind the screen of clouds the sun remained burning, and its piercing rays worked their way through towards the glowing earth.

"There's going to be a thunderstorm," said Ruki quietly.

Kromorejo was working by his side. He was progressing but slowly. Round his foot he had tied a clumsy rag. He had hurt himself on a sharp hidden splinter of wood, and there was a deep wound between two of his toes. It had been suppurating for more than a week, growing bigger and bigger and eating into the red, inflamed flesh.

"Are you in pain?"

"Yes."

"Why don't you ask the mandur for some medicine?"

"If the mandur sees it, he will tell the tuan and then I shall have to go to hospital."

"I am afraid of the doctor," said Ruki.

"I am afraid too. That's why I don't tell the mandur."

They said nothing for a moment. There was a very distant rumble. It came from far behind the forest as though a great beast were growling there. The silence grew heavier, the heat more intense. The cloud masses descended threateningly, still growing and expanding, struggling for room on the sky that had grown too narrow to contain them.

"What do they do to you in the hospital?" asked Ruki.

Kromorejo stretched himself and glanced at the sky. Then he said: "The tuan doctor is very clever. He gives you a medicine, and that makes you die. Then he cuts out some of the inside of your body, and then he makes you alive again."

"Ts . . . ts . . . wah!" Ruki forgot to work.

"But I am afraid," said Kromorejo.

"I am afraid too," said Ruki. "I won't go to hospital either."

"But if the tuan knows you're ill you'll have to go. They send you." And, bending towards Ruki, he whispered dramatically, "I've been there once!"

"Wah!" Ruki looked at Kromorejo aghast, but curious at the same time. "And did the doctor kill you too? And resurrect you afterwards?"

Kromorejo shook his head. "No, not that time.

He made me drink castor oil. And I was given no food. Not for two days. And after that only broth. But Parman came to visit me and he secretly gave me fish and rice. If he hadn't done that, I should most certainly have died. And then I saw how the doctor made a man die in order to cut away his entrails. The blandas think that such things are good for one."

"And aren't they good?"

"But of course not," answered Kromorejo. "There are certain medicines that will help sometimes when one is ill. But if they don't help it proves clearly that Allah thinks one's life has been long enough as it is, and then one must die whether they cut something out of one's body or not. But those blandas have many queer notions like that. Not long ago, but before you arrived, the tuan doctor came to the plantation. They called it inspection. He felt every coolie in turn, all over his body, and he even tapped them, and then he pulled up their eyelids and looked into their eyes."

"Did he look into their eyes? Whatever for?"

"That I do not know. They think that it is good for one."

A sharp flash of lightning cut across the sky. A heavy clap of thunder fell like a blow from a giant's club. They shrank together. In the course of their conversation they had forgotten the sky that hung over them like a dreadful threat. Then Ruki looked up and remarked calmly: "There is going to be a thunderstorm."

"Look out! Here is the tuan," said Kromorejo,

hastily bending down to his work, and hiding his sore foot.

The assistant passed along, followed by the mandur. "If it begins to rain, the coolies must go to the compound," they heard the tuan remark.

"Yes, tuan," replied the mandur.

Just above the forest the sky had become a mass of dark grey. The heat was unbearable. It penetrated their flesh like fiery arrows. Then another red flash zigzagged across the lowering sky. A heavy clap of thunder clanged and echoed. A flame hissed and crackled through the air and sundered the crown of a mighty tree in the forest. The sharp rending sound of the splitting wood mingled with the drum-like roll of the thunder that called up dark echoes from the depths of the forest. This concatenation of noises broke over the earth like growling waves of an angry sea, and again, more quickly than before, a flash of lightning ran over the grey clouds. It grew dark as though suddenly the evening had come. There was no sound now but that of the furious thunder which seemed to castigate the earth and which beat down upon it with such fury that the soil appeared to tremble in its deepest layers.

Through the threatening rumble rose the order: "Home, every one of you! Back to the compound!"

The dismissed coolies at once threw their spades across their shoulders. Their voices rose happy and loud like those of children returning home after school. Along the plantation young wood was growing. They picked large banana leaves and held them over their heads like umbrellas. Those who were wearing jackets took them off, rolled them into small bundles, and placed them on their heads.

All around them forked the lightning. The crackling, hissing red shafts followed one another with ever-increasing speed, till the earth seemed afraid. It seemed to wait all doubled up for each new blow from the burning sky, and for each rolling, shattering clap of thunder. Behind the sharp ruddy light that was kindled afresh every second appeared the monstrous leaden clouds, a threatening dark wall that still continued to grow. Angry tongues of fire spurted from them to seek the trembling earth. Then the wind rose, chasing the dense masses of cloud across the sky, shaping them into dragons, monsters, towers, and finally into a level expanse of flat greyness. It was above the forest that the level surface broke first. It gave way under the mighty pressure of the wind, and a black curtain of water hung between the sky and the tree-tops. The deluge rushed nearer, splashing, swishing, clattering. First there was a vanguard of a few drops—drops that fell like stones. Immediately behind came a moving screen of water which raced on and swallowed up the whole landscape. The noisy onrush of the rain obliterated even the sound of the thunder whose rumblings grew weaker and more distant.

The forest had disappeared. Of paths there was no trace. Nothing remained but a milky white world filled with cataracts of rain. Through this watery chaos marched the coolies like dim spectres, grotesque under the immense leaves with which they shielded their heads. Their calling voices had something singularly dull as though they were extinguished by the immovable rhythm of the vertical columns of rain.

It rained throughout the day and throughout the night. All night long the rain fell over the compound square, a flood of sound that absorbed all other sounds, that seemed to absorb also the consciousness of the coolies.

The day refused to dawn.

The second ton-tong had already sounded with its monotonously warning voice. Still there was no trace of life. Through the darkness that no longer belonged to night the rain continued to fall. It rushed down in straight lines with an even, regular swish. The water fell unhurriedly but with an obstinacy that made one feel it would never cease. Not a voice was heard above the sound of the water, which was everywhere, pouring from the sky on to the earth, clattering on the roofs, rushing down from them to the soil, gurgling in every gutter and ditch, rushing past in the distant river and in the brook, beating down on the forest.

Chilled, their sarongs drawn over their shoulders right up to their chins, the contract coolies sat huddled together on the little porches in front of their huts. Cold and shivering, the dogs and the chickens that had slept with them in their huts remained suffering by their sides. Human beings and animals alike waited in the hope that the time would come when the rain would fall no more, and when out of this endless grey dusk day would at last break. They waited fatalistically, submissively without any notion of time or the hour, since the sun remained invisible.

It continued to rain. A spark of light struggled through the greyness. Still there was no other sound than the swishing, streaming rush of the falling jets of water. It lulled everybody into a hypnotic trance. Men and animals dozed, packed closely together, their eyelids shut in a chilled and morose slumber full of depressing reveries.

The rain continued to pour down for three more hours.

Then suddenly the rain began to fall in drops instead of in sheets, and the drops grew finer and sparser. For one moment it drizzled. Then the wind rose and turned the drizzle into a mist while it tore the massive clouds to ribbons. Like a visitor from another world, a ray of sunshine slipped through all this water in suspense. The dogs shook themselves and began to scratch their mangy spots, and all at once a young cockerel jumped on to the rim of a dustbin and crowed hoarsely.

"It is getting dry," said Ruki.

Kromorejo made no reply. He continued to shudder, hidden in the folds of his vast kaïn.

"What's the matter?" asked Ruki. "Are you ill?"

His companion's only reply was a moan of pain.

"He has a fever," said another man. "He has a wound."

Ruki opened Kromorejo's kaïn and sarong. His foot, from which he had removed the bandage, was swollen into a shapeless thing, and three fiery red streaks ran up his swelling leg. Kromorejo shivered again, and his teeth chattered. Then as the ton-tong began to call he lifted his face. His eyes were full of tears, and under his brown skin the feverish blood was burning.

"Up! To your work! Get out all of you!"

Mandur Amat passed along the huts urging the coolies to greater speed. "Up! To work! To work!"

Slowly they struggled out of their lethargy, removed their sarongs, folded them, and placed them beneath their little pillows. They took their implements and, dressed only in shorts, most of them naked above, they went to their work reluctantly and as slowly as they dared.

Kromorejo remained seated. He was resting his head against the wooden wall, and his eyes were closed.

"Now then, Kromorejo, up! Why aren't you out of the compound? Your gang is at work already."

"I cannot work, mandur."

"Why not? Are you ill?"

"Maybe, mandur. I feel so cold. I cannot work."

"Oh, that's only fancy! It has been raining, and that's why you feel cold. Up, quickly! In a moment the tuan will be here, and then you'll get a thrashing."

Amat had already passed on, inspecting each hut to make sure that no one was hidden away. Kromorejo dropped his kaïn a little, and got up with great difficulty.

"Hs . . . hs . . . hs . . . alas!"

As the blood began to flow again through the

inflamed leg, he moaned softly. For a moment he leaned against the wall, shivering and giddy; then he hobbled into the hut. He tore two strips off an old worn out sarong that was lying there in the dust and the dirt under his couch and began to bandage his foot.

Yes, when he tied the strips very tightly the pain was not so bad. It was better after all to go to work. If the tuan found him here he would have to go to hospital. He groped for his hoe. An old cigarette tin lay beneath his pillow. It contained a little tobacco and a leaf for making a cigarette. It also contained eleven cents, which were all his worldly possessions. He rolled himself a cigarette. Then he took some water from a paraffin tin and drank avidly.

Allah! Allah! How thirsty he was! There was a great fire within his body.

Slowly, shivering and halting at almost every step, then compelling himself to move on again, he hobbled towards the fields.

"Come along!" shouted the mandur from a distance. "Hurry up! Tuan will be here in a moment."

"Yes, mandur."

Before his eyes, everything grew confused: the long rows of young rubber trees, the mimosa that sprouted round them, and the coolies bending down and hoeing at the roots of the trees. His arms seemed leaden and his head was aglow. The blood beat behind his temples. Each time a gust of wind passed over the field he shivered. He worked mechanically without looking up. He failed to notice that he was getting behind the others. Suddenly the stern voice of the assistant startled him from his torpor.

"Hey! You there! Why don't you get on with your work? Can't you see that your mates are far ahead of you?"

Kromorejo looked up and dimly, as in a mist, he perceived the outline of the coolies, and quite close to him the large, threatening figure of the tuan.

"Yes," he brought out, but his teeth chattered so much that he could hardly speak.

The assistant gave him a searching look. "What's the matter? Are you ill?"

"Oh no, tuan, I'm not ill." He began to work desperately, heroically almost, so that the white man might not notice his wound. But the assistant did not allow him to go on.

"Squat!"

Kromorejo squatted. The assistant placed the back of his hand against the brown cheek and was startled at the burning contact. "You're feverish, Kromorejo. Why didn't you report sick this morning?"

"Afraid," said Kromorejo softly, hardly opening his lips.

"Afraid? Why are you afraid?"

"I am afraid of being cut open."

The European shrugged his shoulders impatiently. "You buffalo! If you don't go to the hospital, you'll die."

This opened a new vista of hope before Kromorejo's eyes. It was as though a choice were offered to him. "It does not matter. I am not afraid to die. I am only afraid of the tuan doctor, and I won't drink castor oil."

"Silence, you buffalo! You're not in a position to say won't. Let me see that!" The assistant pointed to the rags round Kromorejo's foot.

Silently he fiddled with the knots. At last he managed to undo them, and as soon as the tight bandage was loosened, the blood began to flow faster through the leg; but he betrayed no pain. He only drew in his breath between his teeth: "Hs . . . hs . . . hs . . ."

The rags dropped off and the leg was bare. He stretched it out before the tuan.

"A wound," was all he said, and he waited resignedly for what would be decided about him.

The assistant drew back with a start at the sight of the hideously inflamed leg. By this time the red streaks ran higher than the knee.

"You ass! You bl . . . fool! I ought really to thrash you as you've never been thrashed before! Amat, mandur Amat!"

"Yes, tuan!"

The other coolies looked up. They were completely indifferent to what was happening. It had nothing to do with their own persons, so why should they be interested in the case?

The assistant pointed with his stick to Kromorejo. "Hadn't you noticed this?"

Only now the mandur paid attention to Kromorejo, bent towards the leg, looked at it for quite a long while, and finally said: "Ts . . . eh!"

"Didn't you know he was ill? What are you mandur for?"

"I thought he was only shamming, tuan."

"I thought . . . I thought! You're just as big a fool as the rest of them. And you a man from town, from Sourabaya, not a yokel from the dessa! You're so old that your moustache has grown on both sides beyond your cheeks, and still you've no more brains than a new contract coolie! Is that why I made you mandur? He must go to the office at once. I expect the ox-cart for the sick will still be there."

"Yes, tuan."

His head bent down, his hands folded on the knob of his stick, Amat received the scolding. Then he accepted the hospital chit for Kromorejo. He stood like this motionless till the tuan had turned his back and walked away. Then he went up to Kromorejo and slapped his face as hard as he could. "You fool! Why didn't you tell me you were ill? You wouldn't do that, no! But to make me stand in shame before the tuan, yes, that's easier, isn't it?"

"But didn't I tell you that maybe I was ill?" replied Kromorejo in self-defence.

"What did you tell me? You told me nothing, and you can shut up."

Amat looked with flaming eyes at the crouching figure. He kicked him in the back, and said: "You just wait till you are back from hospital! I'll find some nice work for you to do. I'll make you remove the coolies' latrines. You understand? And I shan't allow you to use your spade. You'll have to work with your hands. Do you see? With your hands in the dung. Up! Be off! And give this chit to the clerk."

"Yes, mandur."

Kromorejo rose with difficulty and swayed for a moment. "Hs . . . hs . . . alas!"

Amat continued to watch him with venomous eyes. He felt not the slightest impulse to pity for the sick man. He only knew that Kromorejo whom the tuan had put under his authority had somehow eluded complete domination. Kromorejo had made him feel ashamed, had made him ridiculous, and when the coolie, feeling giddy, stopped for a moment with closed eyes, Amat bawled mercilessly at him: "Get a move on! Quicker! Don't stand about like that."

Hobbling and struggling to remain on his feet, Kromorejo made his way towards the office. He dragged himself along with great difficulty. The vertical rays of the sun beat down on him and burned him. Low over the ground hung a steaming heat. The road seemed endless as he followed it, resting from time to time. New clouds piled forebodingly in the sky, threatening to pour down the rain of which they were still full. It was as though the growing heat of the atmosphere made his blood hotter. It rushed madly through his body, and he felt as though his heart would burst. His lips felt dry and hot and burning. His eyes ached, and yet he felt cold, dreadfully cold. The cold was creeping up from his finger-tips towards his heart, like a reptile gorging on his boiling blood.

The ox-cart was still in front of the office. He

handed the chit to the clerk, who ordered him into the cart. Four other sick men were in it already. The driver helped him to get in. Composedly, resignedly, he allowed everything to happen. He hardly noticed that the other patients were giggling at his helplessness. He had ceased to think. He had given up resisting. It was his fate, apparently. Maybe Allah had determined that it was to be like this. After all, he was only orang kontrak, so, if he was ordered to go to hospital, he had to go to hospital. He drew his sarong around him, and leaned his head against the side of the cart.

The cart proceeded slowly, shaking and rattling on its axles. The lazy ruminating oxen seemed to move one step at a time. They were in no hurry. Now and then the cry of the driver broke the silence. The rain had begun again. It dripped through the leaf roof of the cart. Sometimes, when the road was particularly bad and his head dropped away and swayed back against the side with a bang, Kromorejo moaned. But he was unaware of this. The fever had him in its grip, and had closed over him like a boiling, hissing eddy.

II

FIVE weeks passed. Kromorejo had not returned from hospital. His place in the bachelors' hut had been taken by Nur. Nur slept on Kromorejo's mat and on his small greasy pillow. He had also appropriated the cigarette tin with the tobacco and the eleven cents.

"But it belongs to Kromorejo," Ruki had observed diffidently.

Nur had laughed mockingly. "Let it belong to him! He's not coming back, and the mandur said that I am to live here, so now it belongs to me."

Ruki could find no reply to this argument. As he sharpened his spade, he cast a surreptitious glance at Nur.

He was rather afraid of Nur, who came from Sourabaya and had worked as a dock hand in the harbour there. Nur was a veritable crocodile: boastful, vulgar, shameless. He had grown up among the scum that frequented the waterside and made its living loading and unloading the boats. He had got into some kind of trouble and had taken refuge in Deli because the police wanted him. In his veins ran a strain of Madurese blood, which certainly did not contribute to make him any less difficult, intractable, and rebellious.

"Troublesome!" said the mandurs over him, and they kept a close watch on him in the hope of finding him at fault. He was a good deal too ready with his tongue. His ancestors in Madura had never hesitated long about drawing their knives. Nur seemed to have inherited something of this propensity. One could read it in the dark glance of his eyes, in the fold of his obstinate lips. Deep in his heart smouldered a fire that did not flare up, but could not be extinguished. He had been thrashed times without number by the tuans, by the head mandur, and by his own mandur. The under-mandurs dared not touch him. He had spent three months of his first contract year in prison. Prison had not improved him. A prisoner could laze through the day, could smoke, and was given better food than he got when working on the estate. Nur preferred prison to the compound with its eternal compulsion and its regulated life full of rules. Now and then he refused to work. Sometimes he ran away into the virgin forest. There he hid for days till hunger drove him back. He did it in the hope of being sent back to prison. All these lost days he would have to serve at the end of his contract period. But he did not mind. He knew that if he went back to Java worse would befall him. But the assistant had had enough of this. He no longer sent Nur before the magistrate. Instead he had transferred him from section one to section three, because mandur Amat was also from Sourabaya. And Amat made short work of Nur: he thrashed him black and blue. For days he would walk about with an enormously swollen eye. At other times he appeared with blood red weals all over his face. In this condition he would work under sheer compulsion. But a bitter hatred smouldered between the two men from Sourabaya, and it waxed fiercer and fiercer.

"Nur has caught it again," the others would say from time to time, with a grin. But it was a stealthy grin. They would not have dared laugh openly because they realized that, impotent to avenge himself on the mandur Amat, he would cool his hatred upon some one of them.

Ruki had gone outside the hut. He was squatting on the threshold, smoking. He thought of Kromorejo. Kromorejo was certainly dead. A feeling of loneliness stole over his heart. Had not Kromorejo been his mate? Now no one was left. He thought of Sidin and Karimun. Where would they be? Had they managed somehow to return to the campong? Were they guarding their buffaloes on the grassland once more?

He continued to smoke in silence, his thoughts turned inward, motionless, his eyes dreaming. Would he ever return? When his contract time was over, they had told him. Another two years and a month. Two years and a month as the blandas counted it. . . . How many moons would that be? So many, he thought, that it was impossible to reckon. It was as long as for ever. He lost himself in his melancholy meditations. . . . Before him there lay stretched out an expanse of time so vast that he could not see the end of it. . . . It was infinite. It was eternal.

When? Again and again this question awoke in his soul. When? How could one tell? It was far away still, that much he knew. Such was fate, and what could he do against it? He was the weaker one, the foolish one—that was the answer to all these questions. And he plodded on, labouring, performing tasks that were imposed upon him, living as he was compelled to live without knowing, without understanding why.

It was a bright night. A silver moon stood high and still in the crystal clear sky. Now and then a thin wreath of mist stopped as though hooked to the shiny white crescent. Then it slipped away across the transparent blue that was so deep, so mysterious, so immaterial that it had an air of eternity. Over all things that were of the earth lay a deep repose. It was a repose that poured down from the sky with the moonlight, and hung over the empty compound square, over the motionless coconut palms and over the dark dwellings of the coolies. It was a strange peace that lay like a blanket over their dark, unexpressed melancholy.

Near Ruki was Wirio, cooking the evening meal for Sentono and her little boy Païdi. She was squatting, and from time to time she stirred the contents of her wide pan with a black iron spoon. The vegetables sizzled and gurgled in the boiling coconut oil. A sharp reek penetrated Ruki's nostrils. It reminded him of nenneh. How often she had cooked the same dish for him. How often he had sucked up this sauce from his little cup as he sat in their small room on the worn-out mat near the smoky wick surrounded by buzzing mosquitoes. And then every night there had been nenneh's voice, which every evening had said: "Come along! Come to bed!"

It had been a moonlit night when he had laid himself by her side for the last time. He wondered what she was doing now. Maybe she had died too, just like Kromorejo.

Païdi had trotted out of the hut next to Ruki's. He had not a stitch on him, but round his neck hung a string of dirty beads, and at the end of the string dangled a grubby, greasy rag into which had been sewn a fragment of his umbilical cord. It was to protect him from evil spirits. His head was shaven. One long solitary lock of hair hung over his forehead and into his eyes. He shouted in a shrill, childish voice: "Ma! ma! I'm hungry!"

"The food isn't ready yet," snapped Wirio. "Get out of the way. Go and play."

The child looked at her wistfully and picked up the long stalk of a banana leaf.

"Come here, Paidi," Sentono called to him. "I'll make a horse for you."

"Good, Pa."

The child called Sentono father. He remembered nothing of his own father who had perhaps sought for him in vain somewhere far away in Java. His mother had been allotted to Sentono. Now these three belonged together.

Païdi placed himself by the side of Sentono, who had brought out a hatchet from under the pillow in his hut. Now he cut a piece from the stalk and bent it over.

"Find me a coconut leaf."

Païdi looked round, crept over the dusty, dirty ground, and returned in triumph. Sentono cut a bit out of the central vein of the leaf, pushed it through the bent end of the stalk, and fixed it with some fibre.

"That's its head," declared Sentono.

The child observed him solemnly, and repeated without a smile: "That's its head."

While he was thus occupied Sentono hummed: it was a continually repeated motif in a minor key, dark as the silence, peaceful as the moonlight. A little bit of leaf remained on the stalk. He cut it into narrow strips. That was the horse's tail.

"Now it's a horse, do you see?" Sentono presented the stalk to the little boy. Païdi took hold of the hobby horse carefully and held it proudly against his fat, naked, rice-belly, over which the skin was taut as that of a drum.

"Horse!" said Païdi. His black eyes had a warm glow under the lock of hair. Sentono picked up the child and rubbed his nose against its cheek. There was infinite tenderness in this cautious gesture. Then he stood leaning against the doorpost holding the child in his arms and humming again the same tune. In the gaming shed someone was playing the gamelan. Mysteriously melancholy, unerringly rhythmic came the voice of the metal gong. Sentono and Païdi stared together into the moonlight that trickled from the pointed leaves of the coconut palms. Both of them listened to the dark, dripping music. Both were equally serious, equally meek. Sentono drew an indescribable sense of consolation from the frail, childish body in his arms. Paidi, with the horse hanging limp from his little fist, sank into a vague peace because his naked belly was growing so deliciously warm against the bare chest of his foster father.

Nur also had come outside. He was smoking in sombre silence. A figure moved across the moonlit square: a woman's figure. She passed close to Ruki and Nur. It was Saïma. Something moved at the extreme end of the square by the side of the bamboo hedge round the well. Nur raised his head and peered through the uncertain light. His body was tense as that of a panther in ambush. As Saima passed just in front of him he jumped up unexpectedly. She was startled, uttered a shriek, and crossed her forearms over her breast. "Lah-illah-Allah!"

"Where are you going?" Nur's voice was threatening.

She threw up her chin challengingly. She laughed loud and provokingly. "I'm going to the Chinese camp! What do you want with me? I don't belong to you, do I?"

She walked on. From the shadow of the bamboo hedge another shadow detached itself.

"A Chinese," said Ruki almost under his breath.

Nur held his square head rigidly on one side. He was listening intently. Sentono also was listening. Between these two there was for once a link: the link of a violent hatred against a man of another race who was cheating them of their own women. He handed Païdi to his mother and picked up his hatchet. Noiseless as a cat, Nur crept into his hut. He returned with the first spade on which he had chanced to lay hands. It happened to be Ruki's.

Saïma had by now walked past the well at the edge of the compound. The second shadow followed her. Nur and Ruki waited another moment, then, without a sign to one another, without exchanging as much as one word, they walked in the direction of the two shadows. Sentono walked one step behind.

Shamelessly, Saïma shouted in their direction: "What do you men want? It's none of your business!"

They did not answer. A second later several dull thuds fell on the air, and the cries of a man in agony. It was the Chinese shouting in broken Malay: "Have pity! Have pity!"

From all the huts people streamed like ants towards the well.

"Finish him! Finish him! The Chinese pig!"

Their voices rose, jeering. The quiet moonlit night was suddenly filled with terrifying, coarse, bestial sounds. In one second, the dreamy piety of these softly moving people had changed to furious blood lust. Every one of them brandished some weapon—a hatchet, a spade, a log of wood. They shrieked and yelled and laughed like madmen. In this hurricane of voices, the pitiful groans of the Chinese were lost.

"Finish him! Lynch him! Hack him to little bits! We'll teach them to lure away our women!"

A savage madness had seized them, a delirious joy

at the sight of Nur belabouring the Chinese with the handle of the spade.

"Lynch him! Finish him! Hack him to little bits, the Chinese pig!"

The Chinese, who was writhing on the ground like a snake, tried to protect his head with his two hands. Leaning over him stood Nur and Sentono. Nur, drunk with hatred and blood lust, beat him in a blind rage without knowing where he struck. All his pent-up rancour, all his smothered rebellion broke out in a wild surging desire for destruction. Sentono was carried away on the same wave of primitive hatred. This family man, this simple, kindly being was suddenly possessed by a new sense of power which clouded his thoughts. To feel stronger than another was a sensation long unfamiliar to him, and in a second the unaccustomed sensation had turned him into a bestial barbarian. But his hand still hesitated. His eyes sought support in the circle of spectators.

"On with it! Don't be afraid! Kill him!"

They were all shouting excitedly at him. Nur heard the words. They made him laugh. Then he said raucously, "Yes, kill him! What makes you afraid?"

Sentono lifted his terrible weapon and made a wild lunge at the piteously groaning body. One desperate shriek rang across the compound square. From the twitching body issued a jet of blood. At once all the others threw themselves on the victim. Howling and laughing, they hit at him with spades and hatchets, and despatched him as though he had been some dangerous wild beast that had at last been cornered.

Blood gushed everywhere. It poured from the hideous gaping wounds of the quivering body. The earth drank greedily until it was sodden and smoking with blood.

The body had ceased to twitch, but still they hacked and struck at it, insatiable, yelling, wild with a perverted sense of power. They wanted to kill, but more than the one man. All the others, all those of that tougher, cleverer race that was different, strong, and wealthy. They not only wanted to kill, but to maim, to destroy. While their brown hands tore asunder the yellow flesh, they called upon Allah. There was blood on their faces, on their naked bodies, between the toes of their bare feet. Close by, the women and the children stood huddled together, watching with approval the surging mass of men.

As suddenly as they had gone mad, the men resumed their calm. Their long smouldering hatred and resentment had been quenched. They were pacified. They became quiet, self-possessed, circumspect as before. Over their faces spread once more the unruffled calm that hid their lawless, merciless blood lust. They turned as if they had been one to go back to their huts. But just then they heard mandur Amat's voice telling them to stay where they were. In silence they stood round the body lying there in the soft moonlight on the gory, trampled earth.

"Who did this?" asked Amat threateningly. But the threat in his voice was nothing more than a display of his authority. Had he not stood in the shadow watching the jeering multitude? Had he not seen the murder from a distance? And had not his blood rejoiced in unison with theirs at this destruction? The victim was a Chinese, merely a Chinese. Serve him right. What was he doing here unless he was seducing the coolie women?

But appearances must be kept up. He was mandur. He must be severe, and besides he had to clear himself. He must see to it that when the inquiry took place on the morrow no shadow of complicity could be cast upon him.

"Who did it? Who murdered the Chinese?"

They remained silent. Some of them surreptitiously wiped the blood from their hatchets with their fingers and cast stealthy glances at Sentono.

"Now then, tell me who did it." Amat's voice was loud and important.

Suddenly Nur remarked cynically: "All of us. We did it all together. How can the mandur ask such a question? A man cannot lynch a Chinese by himself. Doesn't the mandur know that yet?" Nur smiled insolently. The others endeavoured to suppress their appreciative grins. Through Amat's hot blood passed a feeling hotter still. He realized that he had been made ridiculous before other men, which is the greatest shame that can befall a man. A long passionate look full of hatred fell from his eyes upon Nur.

"Home!" he said curtly.

They dispersed quietly. Behind them walked Amat, who knew that the police would be able to make neither head nor tail of the affair. What Nur had said would be accepted. All of them together had lynched the Chinese. One cannot well put all the coolies of a section into prison. Who would do the work? And the white men did not mind so very much if there was just one Chinese less. Only . . . of course if there were proof positive, definite witnesses against one or two men . . .

Suddenly he turned round. He had perceived light footsteps behind him.

"Who is there?"

"I, mandur . . . Saïma."

"What do you want?"

"Ruki murdered the Chinese, mandur. I saw it. I walked with the Chinese towards his camp, and then there came Ruki with Nur and Sentono. They all hit him, but Ruki killed him. I saw it myself, and I will bear witness before the Controller. I will swear to it."

Revenge blazed in her eyes. She still remembered how Ruki had once cheated her. She still nursed hatred against him.

The mandur looked down at her.

"Go home!" he said severely. "You are lying. You are just telling a story. The gossip of a hussy . . . No one will believe it. Certainly not the Controller. If you have to bear witness, you will bear witness against the person I tell you to accuse and against nobody else. If you don't do as I tell you, you'll have trouble with me. Do you understand?"

She hesitated a moment.

"*Do* you understand?"

"Yes, mandur."

"Home!"

She walked ahead of him across the square. She realized that she would have to bear witness. She also realized that Amat had some personal insult to avenge. And Amat was mandur. His vengeance therefore had first claim. She would bear witness against whomever she was told. They would place the Koran on her head, and she would take the oath to speak the truth. If it made Allah angry, she could not help it. She would act under the orders of the mandur. The mandur was the stronger.

Amat followed her in deep meditation. A fierce light had gone up in his dark thoughts. He had Nur in his power now. Now he could make Nur pay for all the trouble he had given—and for this last insult when Nur had made him ridiculous before his subordinates. He would compel Saïma to bear witness against him. And not Saïma alone. Ruki also, and Sentono. He paused. Nur was squatting with a tin of water by his side. He was washing the handle of Ruki's spade. Without lifting his eyelids he looked at the mandur, but there was nothing in his attitude to betray that he had seen Amat. Amat took another step, and stood still without speaking a word. There was a deep hostile silence between the two men. At last the mandur asked: "Why are you washing your spade?"

"It is not my spade," answered Nur curtly.

"Whose is it then?"

"Ruki's."

"But why are you washing it then?"

"I am helping Ruki." Nur's voice remained hostile. Again a silence, like a cloud of wicked thoughts, fell between them. Then Amat bent over Nur's hand and pointed to a spot on the handle of the spade.

"That is blood."

Nur uttered a short challenging laugh. Then he asked: "And supposing it were blood?"

Amat lingered another second. Then he walked away. He had not said another word. From beneath his eyelids Nur followed him across the square that was bathed in moonlight. It was almost as light as in the daytime. Only the quiet deep blue quality of the light proclaimed that it was night. Then came, clear and distinct, the sound of the ton-tong. It was nine o'clock and bed-time.

Nur rose and went inside. There was no visible trace of his smouldering hatred. Ruki was already lying on his couch.

"Here's your spade," said Nur, throwing down the tool. Then with a laugh he continued: "Sentono killed him like a pig, the rotten Chinese."

Ruki's dark eyes glittered in the faint glimmer of the oil lamp. "Pig," he said, and his voice sounded very like Païdi's when he said: "Horse!"

Two of the other bachelors entered.

"Where is Iman?" asked Nur.

"He has to help carry the corpse to the tuan's house," they said with a grin.

Then they were all silent. They listened to the squeaking and squealing of the rats, to the buzz of the mosquitoes. And they fell asleep as an animal falls asleep, contented, unconscious, unaware of its own hideous cruelty.

III

KROMOREJO had at last returned from hospital. He hobbled over the compound square on a primitive crutch roughly hewn out of a piece of wood. One of his legs had been amputated above the knee.

"Ts . . . eh!" shouted the coolies in amazement. "Kromorejo has come back!" But they could not help laughing, and, pointing to his stump, they shouted: "Eh! They've cut off his leg. Now he's a cripple," and in a twinkling they had nicknamed him Si Buntung, the stump.

Kromorejo was deeply humiliated. It is shameful to lose a limb. It makes people laugh at one, and to be laughed at is the worst opprobrium. He hobbled to his hut, where he found Ruki.

"Ts . . . eh! Kromorejo!" exclaimed Ruki. "But I thought you must be dead."

"I'm not dead," replied Kromorejo, "but they have cut off my leg."

He sat down on a couch and displayed his mangled stump. Ruki clicked his tongue in amazement. "Ts . . . ts . . . ts! No . . . but I say!"

Kromorejo sat with drooping head.

"In the campong I should have died," he said, "but I'd rather have died. That's what I told the tuan doctor. But that made him angry, and then he made me fall asleep, and afterwards he brought me back to life again. What was I to do? Once you are a contract coolie, you must let them do what they like, even if they order you to have your leg cut off."

Ruki made no reply. What could he say? He could only repeat what Kromorejo had said: "Once you are a contract coolie. . . ."

Kromorejo stood up and fumbled under the pillow in search of his cigarette tin.

"Nur took it," said Ruki.

Kromorejo ruminated. "Nur? From section one?"

"Yes, he sleeps here. He took your sleeping mat and your pillow too. He has sold your sleeping mat. Why didn't you take all your things with you to the hospital?"

"I was ill." That was all Kromorejo had to say. He accepted the event. Nur had made use of circumstances when they were favourable to him. Not to have done so would have been stupid.

"Yesterday we killed a Chinese," remarked Ruki.

Kromorejo was not listening. He had been under contract a year longer than Ruki, and in his first year they had killed seven Chinese. There was nothing very remarkable about killing one.

"I could go back to Java," he said, "but I feel ashamed."

Ruki looked at him. "Home?" he asked, "to Java?"

"Yes."

It made them both silent, this mention of home. They squatted straight up opposite each other, their hands in their laps. Kromorejo's stump, mangled and blunt, stuck out from beneath his sarong. They both held a cigarette between their fingers. Now and then they carried it to their mouths and inhaled the smoke with a deep long breath. The heavy sweetish odour of native tobacco hung round them. Their quiet faces were smooth masks of rigid, passive reflection. Behind these, deep and invisible, lived their unexpressed nostalgia. Kromorejo passed his hand over his stump, and said: "But I prefer to stay here. I shall ask the tuan whether I may stay. Perhaps I can become an orderly in the office."

"So you are not returning?"

"I should feel ashamed to return to my dessa like this. They would all laugh at me. I am poor, and maimed."

"Do you mean to remain orang kontrak until you die, then?"

"Am I not used to being nothing but a contract coolie?"

Ruki did not answer. He thought that Kromorejo was right. One could not go home poor and maimed.

"If it is one's fate . . ." said Kromorejo in a quiet resigned voice. It formed a bridge over a deep chasm, a balm for a wound too severe almost to be borne—nassip: fate. With the aid of this one word, he was able to accept his destiny, now as before. Desire for his dessa, for the freedom of Java was repressed deep within him and for ever. Without a word of complaint, he gave up the land of his birth: it was nassip!

Both of them knew all the implications of the word. But they did not talk about them. They had words only for concrete things. Abstract ideas were communicated from one to the other by those glances half-hidden behind their downcast eyelids, by that mysterious smile that was yet not a smile which played about their lips. They found expression in that heavy, impenetrable silence which was the essence of the puzzling nature of these Javanese coolies and made them at the same time the simplest, most complete philosophers and the cruellest, most horrible children.

Kromorejo was allowed to stay. He was made watchman of the rice shed of section one. He hobbled into the hut to bring the news to Ruki.

"Come with me, mate . . . I have a note for the tuan of section one, and you're to bring back the reply with you."

"Good."

"Will you carry my pillow for me?"

Ruki looked at Nur who sat smoking by Iman's side on the couch that had formerly belonged to Kromorejo.

"Come on," said Kromorejo. "Take it away. It's my pillow."

Nur's face remained expressionless, but his pupils slid towards the other corners of his eyes. Ruki still hesitated.

"Do take it," said Nur sharply and contemptuously. Ruki felt ashamed. He knew that Kromorejo and Iman were grinning at him, although they too were afraid of Nur.

"But am I not already taking it?" he asked, grabbing at it hastily.

"Perhaps he'll be allowed to borrow it one day if ever he has money for a woman," remarked Nur insinuatingly.

The blood rushed hotly to Ruki's cheeks. It showed through the brown skin. Nur got up and stood directly in front of Ruki. Iman and Kromorejo looked on with great interest. The two men stood opposite one another in silence, almost touching one another, waiting to see who would be the first to begin the fight. They stood there as though they were measuring each other's strength, each other's agility. Then Nur smiled offensively.

"Well, what do you want?"

There was no fight. Their antagonism died down again without finding expression. Only the glowing ash remained after the momentary shooting up of the flame. But it continued to smoulder in their hearts. The day would certainly come when it would flare up again. Then the insult would have to be paid for.

Ruki snatched the pillow. It was ragged, greasy, and dirty. But it was Kromorejo's only property. Together they went to section one. It was an hour's walk and Kromorejo did not move easily. He was not yet skilful in the handling of his crutch. It was dark when they arrived. They waited near the annexe of the assistant's house. The house-boy took in the note.

From the kitchen came the ruddy glow of the paraffin lamp and the fire. Inside a woman was cooking. Ruki peered in inquisitively. He recognized Karminah. He went nearer to the window.

"Eh! Karminah! How are you?"

Karminah looked up, trying to penetrate the darkness outside. "Who's that?" she asked sharply, and in her voice there was a new certainty, a new determination that made Ruki draw back.

He replied gently: "It's Ruki."

She came outside and put her hands on her hips. "What, you contract scum? Don't you know your manners? Can't you squat down when you are in the courtyard of the tuan's house? Quick, down with you!"

Startled, Ruki squatted down. Karminah remained on the doorstep for another moment looking down at him contemptuously. "And you dare come here like this without a jacket, in your naked skin?"

Ruki lowered his head in shame. He had no jacket. How could he afford to buy one when all his wages went to the free woman who cooked his food, and the few cents that remained were lost in gambling? If ever he chanced to have a little money, the older coolies stole it.

Karminah, back in the kitchen, shouted brief, quick orders to the water-carrier who was fanning the fire by blowing through a bamboo cane. Ruki contemplated her stealthily. She had grown fatter. She wore a white jacket with lace. Four large English sovereigns held it together. A gold pin gleamed in her hair, and she walked on slippers, not bare-footed.

She need no longer labour with the spade, Ruki meditated slowly. No heavy work for her, no blows. The tuan had made her a housekeeper and she slept with him. A good job, and she had risen in the world: she was allowed to scold a contract coolie. It was fate. Nassip. She had been luckier than he. He had nothing except the shorts in which he worked—not even a sleeping mat or a pillow. He seldom had a woman. His body had grown lean. It was seamed with scars from the wounds he had received while at work. So were his legs. Nassip. And the fate of the one was different from the fate of the other.

"Here! The reply." The water carrier put a note in his hand. To Kromorejo he said: "You can go to the compound."

They rose together. At the garden gate their ways parted. They took leave with a brief word, hardly looking at one another.

Ruki strolled back unhurriedly. He walked with downcast head. His heart was heavy within him. Kromorejo had talked of Java. He had seen Karminah, and suddenly he saw also his nenneh, the buffalo, the campong. In the darkness a tranquil dream picture rose before him: the grasslands, the volcano, the paddy that was ripening and growing yellow around and below his tent on tall stakes. He saw the blue sky, and, planing round in circles, the bird of prey at which he had shouted: "Ouie!

Ouie!" The clouds drifted overhead towards the crater of the volcano. Evening was falling. The flying-foxes fluttered homeward. He saw the river, the campong square, the praying men, and then nenneh, who called him from the circle of quiet smokers to eat his food and go to sleep. There was Supinah and after the paddy had been cut she would . . . But he had not cut the paddy. Who had gathered the harvest? Nenneh? And who had taken Supinah?

Ruki had left the road. He was walking straight across the new plantation towards the forest. He went on like a sleep-walker. The pale sickle of the moon was standing against the immense expanse of heaven. A few stars shone with a watery diamantine glitter. The earth lay round him, dark, lonely, and seemingly derelict. He went through the darkness alone with his murmuring dream. Ahead of him rose the powerful trees. the forest that loomed higher and higher out of the intense black darkness. It moved towards him. It absorbed him. And suddenly the earth around him shook off death. Thousands of sounds rustled and whispered from out the dense vegetation. A life, manifold and mysterious, kept pace with his soundless tread. Without hesitation he followed the narrow path cut by the Chinese woodmen. It led towards the heart of the forest. He scratched himself on the spiny arms of the rattan. Once he trod on a sharp thorn. Drops of blood lay where his foot had passed. But he noticed none of these accidents. He hardly realized whither he was going. Something greater than himself called. It was the volcano, the grassland that called him, and all the sunny days when he had sat on the mighty body of the buffalo glowing with warmth. His only response was to plunge deeper and deeper into the forest towards the round open space where the Chinese had been sawing planks. There stood a small empty hut. He crept into it, and squatted down. Clutched in his fist was the note for his tuan. He squatted quietly, his arms and legs crossed, his head against his knee, in the attitude of an unborn man. He was sitting on the heated soil from whose warmth the greedy life was growing. Mosquitoes buzzed around him and sucked themselves full of his blood. Ants dropped down upon him and stung his feet. The shrill song of cicadas pierced his ears.

Through the hearts of mouldering tree trunks worms ate and bored their way. Over his head monkeys slumbered restlessly at the thinnest end of the swaying branches. Sometimes their sleep grew deeper, their bodies became inattentive and wavered over the deep, deadly dangerous darkness; but just before falling they woke up with a startled scream and recovered their hold, moaning in the dream that was again closing their eyes. Animals peered through the dark, mating, devouring, attacking, and defending themselves. They called to their mates, grunted and growled over a groaning prey or shrieked in their last agony. Or, mute and frightened, they brought forth new life.

Sometimes the sum of all these sounds was so startling that it made Ruki shiver. But he was not really afraid. He listened to that seething life struggle without realizing that, in this one night of groaning and murder, life perished a thousand times and was re-born a hundred thousand.

He thought of his former existence, of the planting of the paddy, of how he had lain in the sunshine piping into a flute made out of a rice straw. In those days, every day had been good. And life itself had been good then. It had been exquisite, beautiful—without mandur, without ton-tong, without compulsion: existence as Allah had arranged it for men. And he wanted that life again.

Unconsciously, his soul had broken away from the immobility which civilization had clamped on him. A sudden longing for freedom had driven him into the inaccessible wilderness of the forest. There he had squatted down. Hunger gnawed at his entrails; but his heart was at rest, because he cherished sweet, foolish dreams of never returning to work. He thought he had fled for ever from the compound, from the ton-tong, from the mandur, from the tuan.

Then he fell asleep.

## IV

IN section three, the assistant was calling over the roll. The sun had not yet risen. A pale faint light was beginning to penetrate the darkness, and the damp, chilling wind of dawn blew through the garden where the coolies squatted in long rows. In the shadows and the mist of early morning they seemed like dark, uncertain spectres. The assistant himself stood in the circle of light cast by a lamp which the boy held up before him. From his circle of light he looked at the coolies who were squatting two by two. He counted them rapidly, gang by gang, as they were assembled for work. As soon as a gang was complete, it was allowed to go away at once in charge of its mandur.

"To work!" he said each time, and the order fell sharply into the grey silence. Only the sick remained behind waiting to be given chits for the hospital.

It was the beginning of a long day of toil, a difficult beginning since everyone was still sleepy and out of temper. For the coolies especially it was difficult: they had to squat, shivering and shrammed with cold, waiting till they were told to rise and go to their work.

From mandur Amat's gang a man was missing.

"Still Ruki, mandur?"

"Yes, tuan."

Amat joined his fingers beneath the sun-helmet which he held in one hand.

"He can't have found his way to one of the other compounds by mistake, can he?" asked the assistant. "He's still rather stupid. He hasn't been here long."

"Perhaps he has found his way to one of the other compounds," said the mandur with Oriental courtesy, for it would have been rude to contradict a superior, "but I think," he continued, "that he has run away. Maybe he is in the forest."

"Perhaps," said the assistant, and, bending over his note-book he wrote something. Then, turning towards the mandur, he said: "Your men can go too, Amat."

The coolies looked up, expecting to hear the mandur repeat the tuan's order. But Amat did nothing of the kind. He took a step towards the assistant, and began to speak in a whisper: "Tuan must not be angry with me, but I want to say something. It's this business about Ruki. Maybe someone incited Ruki to run away."

Amat remained standing very modestly, his head bent down a little and his hands still folded underneath his helmet. The assistant looked suspiciously at the meek, bowing figure. What was Amat's game?

"Who would have incited Ruki to run away?"

Amat looked up again, and said, in particularly soft tones: "If tuan will allow it, I should like to detain three coolies. They are Nur, Sentono, and

Saïma. Meanwhile the others could go to their work."

"Right!"

Amat turned towards his gang of coolies. "Sentono and Nur, stay here. The others can go to their work."

Only Nur glanced up. The others neither betrayed nor felt the slightest astonishment, interest, or curiosity.

"Manduress Minah!"

"Yes, tuan."

"Detain Saïma. The others can go."

"Yes, tuan."

"Sit down with the others, Saïma."

Saïma stood up and then crouched down again a few paces from Nur and Sentono. There was a period of silence while the other men and women marched quietly away out of the garden.

The first red morning light broke through the dusk. The boy took away the lamp and blew it out. The assistant frowned. He was waiting for the communication the mandur had to make. His glance rested for a moment on the three squatting figures: their faces were closed and enigmatic.

"Well, Amat, so you believe someone has put Ruki up to running away? And who do you think has done that?"

Amat glanced over his shoulder. Nearest to him sat Nur. With his finger he was drawing patterns in the sand, but behind his unperturbed face he was all rigid attention. Amat was aware of this. He chose his words carefully.

"Someone perhaps who is afraid that Ruki might bear witness against him," was all he said.

Nur looked up quickly, but lowered his head again at once.

"Bear witness? What about?"

Amat cleared his throat. His drooping shoulders and his bent head made a perfect picture of submission and humility.

"Has not a Chinese been murdered in our compound?" he asked softly.

"Oh *that* case! Yes." The assistant hesitated a moment. A quick glance passed between Amat and Nur. It was charged with hatred and vengefulness. In the growing light of the new day the silence was heavy and tense. Underneath it lay the secret, seething struggle of these two men. In that hot, fermenting soil fanaticism and murder flourish like a vicious parasite.

"And you think Ruki knows who the main culprit is?"

"Perhaps Ruki knows it."

"And the others don't know it?"

"Perhaps the others know it too."

"Why should Ruki alone have run away then?"

Amat hesitated a moment, pondering on this difficult question. Then, with a faint smile, he said: "Maybe he is afraid. He is still a new coolie."

The assistant's thoughts went back to the police inquiry on the estate. All the coolies had been lined up in a row. Each of them in turn had given the same reply: "I don't know. I don't know. . . ."

"But when they were before the police they all of them denied all knowledge."

"Afraid!"

"And of whom were they afraid?"

'Of the culprit, perhaps. Probably he is a dangerous coolie . . ."

Nur shifted his position.

"Now I don't want any of your long stories, mandur. Tell me who did it."

Amat wiped his mouth and looked behind him at the three squatting figures.

"The witnesses . . ." said Amat, beginning very slowly and holding the eyes of Sentono and Saïma with a steady glance, "the witnesses say that Nur did it."

"Not true!" exclaimed Nur passionately. "I didn't do it."

"Silence!" ordered the assistant. Then, turning towards the mandur: "So it's Nur? Who can bear witness to that?"

"Ruki can bear witness to it. And Saïma and Sentono also. They were present all three of them when Nur gave the death blow to the Chinese."

"Sentono!"

"Yes, tuan."

"Did Nur kill the Chinese?"

Sentono hesitated. His eyes under their downcast lids glanced anxiously at Nur.

"Answer!" barked Amat.

"Maybe Nur killed him," said Sentono softly.

The assistant was losing patience. "Maybe! Maybe! That's no reply."

"Yes, tuan."

"It isn't true," shouted Nur. "I didn't do it. He did it himself. Saïma can bear witness to that, and Ruki too."

"Silence, you!" said the assistant curtly.

Sentono stared at the ground.

"Did you not do it yourself, Sentono?"

"No, tuan. I didn't do it." His denial was scarcely audible.

The assistant looked sternly at the three coolies. "You, Sentono, did you yourself see Nur kill the Chinese?"

Sentono realized by now that it was a choice of himself or Nur. He also realized that Amat meant Nur to be picked out as the culprit. True, Sentono was afraid of Nur. But he was still more afraid of the mandur, and now there was suddenly this accusation, about to fall either on Nur or on himself. Behind the accusation rose the figures of the tuan, the tuan besar, the judge. Once he had been brought before the judge because he had run away. He was seized by nervous fear. In his anxiety he felt certain of nothing except one thing: he must accuse Nur. Only by so doing could he attain that safety at which he clutched blindly and desperately.

"I saw it myself," he said with decision. This time he spoke clearly, and from that moment martyrdom itself could not have forced him to alter his assertion.

"And why didn't you say so when the police examined you?"

"Afraid!" said Sentono, repeating the mandur's word.

For one moment a smile of satisfaction passed over Amat's lips. He knew that he had won the day. He no longer looked at Nur, who sat there like a caged, snarling tiger.

"Saïma!"

"Yes, tuan."

"Did you see who killed the Chinese?"

"Yes, tuan."

"Tell me who did it, but think well before you speak. Remember that the murderer may be hanged."

Hanged! The word lay heavy on the silence. It was a word that belonged to the blandas. The coolies did not realize what it implied. Some of them knew that it was connected with death, but death was not a terrifying idea. They were much more terrified of the tuan besar, or of the office from which sometimes there came such a flood of dreadful curses.

"Well, Saïma?"

She cast a glance at Amat. His stern eyes met hers threateningly.

"Nur . . ." she whispered almost inaudibly.

"Why do you tell me this only now? You told the police you knew nothing."

"Afraid!" she said quietly.

"Of whom were you afraid?" the assistant asked sharply. She was silent. She did not know what to reply. Now of whom was it that she ought to have been afraid? If she gave the wrong answer, mandur Amat would thrash her. She had not forgotten that.

"She was afraid of Nur, of course," said Amat. "Nur beat her once before."

"That is not true," said Nur, trying to defend himself. "I didn't do it. The manduress Minah beat her because . . ."

"Silence!" the assistant said severely. "You've always been too ready to talk, and you still throw your accusations right and left, even against the manduress."

"I didn't do it!" Nur insisted angrily.

"Silence! Presently, when you are before the judge, you will be able to defend yourself." The assistant turned again towards Saïma.

"So you were afraid of Nur?"

"Yes, tuan."

"Why were you afraid?"

"Because he had beaten me," she repeated obediently.

"And the manduress Minah?"

"Yes, she also beat me once. But she is my manduress. But Nur beat me too. . . ." There was now in her voice the same passionate determination as in that of Sentono. She had told a lie, and now she would rather die than make herself ridiculous in the eyes of others by admitting that it was a lie.

"Nur threatened that he would kill me, just as he killed the Chinese. He was angry because I went with the Chinese and did not want to go with him. But he never pays. . . ." By now she had mixed up Nur and Ruki. Only one thing stood out clearly in her confused mind: a man had cheated her, and now she could take vengeance on a man.

The assistant meditated awhile. 'So after all it's a brawl over a woman of the most obvious kind,' he thought. 'Saïma goes with a Chinese. Both Nur and Amat are jealous of the Chinese and also of each other. Nur begins by avenging himself on the Chinese, whereupon Amat avenges himself by denouncing Nur. And now Saïma has an opportunity to avenge the murdered Chinese.'

However, he continued his interrogation: "Are you sure that it was not Sentono who killed him?"

"No, Nur gave him the death blow. He killed him with a hatchet."

Nur looked up. At last his sombre face had come to life.

"I had no hatchet with me," he said. "I had a spade. It was Sentono who had a hatchet."

"For once he speaks the truth," said Amat, and a cunning little smile played about his mouth. "Saïma made a mistake: he did not have a hatchet, he had a spade. But it was not his own spade; he had Ruki's spade. That's the point—he took Ruki's spade so that Ruki might be blamed, if anything came to light. I think that is why Ruki was afraid and ran away. Because there are still blood stains on the handle of Ruki's spade, although Nur tried to wash them off." Amat waited one second, then he added triumphantly: "I myself saw Nur washing Ruki's spade."

Nur made a quick movement.

"Is that so?" asked the assistant. "Did the mandur really see you washing Ruki's spade?"

Nur hesitated.

"Yes . . . tuan. That is true, but . . ."

"Now tuan sees," said Amat, and his ugly little

smile showed once more. "Why otherwise should Nur wash Ruki's spade? And when he found that the blood stains would not wash off, then surely he frightened Ruki and made him run away!"

Nur bowed his head. He knew that he was defeated. This time the mandur had won.

"Where is Ruki's spade?" asked the assistant.

"In my room," said Amat. "When Ruki ran away, I took possession of his spade. Then I saw there were blood stains on the handle. I thought Ruki must be the murderer. So I began to ask questions, and by this means I found out the truth. Therefore it will be a good thing if the police lock Nur up. Besides he makes all the other coolies bad."

The assistant knew that this assertion at any rate was by no means unfounded. He sent his boy to the compound to fetch the spade.

It was full daylight now. The sun was climbing rapidly and the heat was growing. The three coolies continued to squat in silence. Sentono and Saïma now and then peeped at the mandur, who kept them under the spell of his dark eyes. Timidly they avoided his glance, trying to protect themselves against the cunning which had moved matters in exactly the direction he wanted them to go. Nothing frightened them more than cunning. It was a power against which they felt helpless. An invisible power from which there was no protection.

The boy returned and politely handed the spade to the assistant. Amat approached and with a courteous but triumphant gesture pointed to the dark stain on the handle. The assistant nodded. The whole case appeared to be as clear as daylight.

"Have you anything further to say?" he asked Nur.

"I never did it," muttered Nur. "It was Sentono who did it."

"But here are the witnesses, and here is the proof."

"I didn't do it," repeated Nur obstinately. "The mandur wants to blacken me."

This angered the assistant. "Lying! Impertinence! That's quite in your line. You're always giving trouble, first in section one and now here. And then in Java. . . . You had a spot of trouble there too, didn't you? It's about time you were put in your place, my man."

Then, turning towards the mandur: "Take these two people to their work, mandur. Nur will come with me to the office."

"Yes, tuan."

Amat enveloped Nur in one final glance. Then he turned away silently. Saima and Sentono put their spades over their shoulders, and went off to join their respective gangs.

V

RUKI spent seventeen days in the forest. He lived on wild bananas and roots. After darkness had fallen he crept to the different compounds and to the neighbouring Malay campongs and stole as many eatables as he could. These seventeen days turned him into an experienced thief and backwoodsman. His face was swollen with mosquito bites. There was a large wound in his leg. He was dirty and unkempt. In the daytime, hidden behind a dense curtain of creepers, he looked at the fields where in the distance he could see the bending figures of the coolies. They laboured on, toiling at the task which was never done, and always began afresh precisely where it had ended. From the distance, vague and indistinct as a sound from the past, came the call of the ton-tong.

Now they had to eat. And now they had to go home. Presently, at nine o'clock, they would have to go to bed. Had to, always had to. No, he was never going to return. He was happier in the forest, though the rattan thorns tore at his flesh, though the mosquitoes and the ants devoured his body. He was free, free as he had been all his life in Java. He slept as long as he wanted, and when he woke up he continued to lie in the derelict hut of the Chinese woodcutters. He lay with his hands beneath his head, just as he had lain in the old days when he was watching over the paddy. The only difference was that here he could not see the sky. Nothing but dense foliage was visible above his head. But he did not mind. In the canal that passed through the wood he constructed little dams and caught small fish of all kinds which he roasted over a wood fire. Never since he had become a contract coolie had he lived so well. He meditated in contentment on his new way of living. A monkey jumping from branch to branch attracted his attention. Ruki saw that it was a female, and that she was carrying a young one. It clung to the belly of its mother and uttered soft high-pitched shrieks each time its mother jumped.

"Hr . . . hr . . ." shouted Ruki in order to startle her. Frightened by the presence of a human being, she raced away. Ruki laughed, as he had laughed once when he had driven away the bird of prey just as it was dropping to earth. Ruki's voice, and the angry protests of the monkey, sounded loudly through the silence of the forest. They covered the sound of steps, to which Ruki was oblivious. A hand moved the undergrowth a little on one side.

"Oh, so that's where you are!"

Ruki shrank away, just as frightened by this man as the monkey had been frightened by him. Behind him stood an agent of the tuan besar.

"What's the matter? Did I startle you?" he asked with a grin.

"I didn't hear you coming," said Ruki.

"You must come along with me. . . . I've been searching for you these seventeen days."

Ruki looked at him. Freedom had restored his sense of personal dignity. "I won't," he said darkly.

"Come along now, none of your tricks. What do you want in the forest? You'll have to come back some time anyhow. It isn't so easy to run away from a contract. Come along! You'd better come with me. It's my orders that I'm to take you back. So why should you make it difficult for me? How will that help you?"

For a moment Ruki stared sullenly in front of him. Then he rose and followed the agent. They took the path across the fields. It was early still, and the dew had not yet dried. Amicably they walked along one behind the other.

"Am I to go straight back to the compound?" asked Ruki.

Without looking round, the agent replied: "I've got to take you to the tuan besar's office, and probably you'll be sent to prison."

Ruki was afraid. He thought of the office building, and the huge figure of the manager rose before his imagination.

"Will the tuan besar beat me?"

The agent shrugged his shoulders. "Who can tell?" he said with Oriental fatalism. "If he is to beat you, he will beat you."

To Ruki this was a completely satisfactory reply. Of course, if they beat you, they beat you. Nassip. It all depended on your fate. He resigned himself in advance. What else could he do?

"The police have taken Nur away," remarked the agent.

"Nur? Why?"

"Because he killed the Chinese."

Ruki made no comment. He knew that it was Sentono and not Nur who had done the murder. But he kept his counsel. It was none of his business. If the police had taken Nur away, that was nothing to do with him. And if Nur was in prison, it was Nur's affair, Nur's nassip.

"Would you like to smoke?" The agent stopped, made himself a cigarette, and offered the tobacco and a leaf.

Ruki rolled himself a cigarette, and then they walked on, chatting in a friendly way. So long as no tuan was present, the agent saw no reason to display his authority. Why should he do so? He had no quarrel with Ruki, had he? It was not his business if Ruki had run away. Much he cared. Of course, when they came before the tuan besar, he would have to show then that he knew his job.

"You are to be agent, Ali," the tuan besar had said one day. "Yes, tuan besar," he had replied. Of course, what else was he to answer? It was his nassip to be chosen as agent. How could one say to the tuan besar, I don't want to? "And you can be as hard with the coolies as you like. That'll make them frightened of you." "Yes, tuan besar." But it was a pleasant job. He no longer had to dig and labour on the soil. He sauntered along the road for hours on end, he gossiped in the compounds; and meanwhile he kept his eyes open for runaways. It was, after all, only nassip whether one caught them or not. Where was one to seek for them if one did not know where they were hiding? Now to-day he surely would not have discovered Ruki had he not happened to go to the canal to see whether there were any fish to be caught.

"You will have to bear witness against Nur, to say that he killed the Chinese."

"I?" asked Ruki, amazed. "Why?"

"Because you saw it happen. Mandur Amat declares that you saw Nur kill him, and Sentono and Saïma have also borne witness against Nur. They have both sworn to it."

Once more Ruki made no comment. He would have to bear witness? Good: if mandur Amat wanted it to be so. . . . He had been frightened of both of them, of Nur and of the mandur. Now, as Nur had gone, only the mandur remained. He who was the stronger could always arrange matters as he chose.

They were by now near the office. Ruki, apprehensive, began to slacken his pace, and Ali deemed that the time had arrived to display his power.

"Hey!" he shouted so loudly that his voice could be heard far away, and certainly by the manager. "Hey, you buffalo. You think you can run away, do you? But you can't even walk. You've been here more than a year, and yet you don't know that you mustn't run away into the forest. Just wait! The tuan besar hasn't started on you yet. He'll give you such a thrashing. He'll gouge your eyes out. Probably he'll murder you. Move on! A little quicker! For seventeen days I've done nothing but look for you, you son of Satan! Throw away that cigarette! Who gave you permission to smoke?"

Ruki quietly threw down his cigarette end. He accepted the agent's scolding imperturbably, taking it in the same spirit in which it was meant. Ali happened to be agent, and it was his job to act as he did. If he did not behave like that, the tuan besar would be angry with him.

When they reached the office, Ruki squatted down. Now and then he glanced at the little door, feeling rather depressed and wondering what sudden danger to him it concealed. Ali said a word to the clerk, and pointed at him. Suddenly he shrank into himself: the colossal figure of the manager had appeared at the window. Ruki's heart began to beat fast and loud. He breathed with difficulty. In the mortal fear which suddenly sprang up in him, he seemed to see everything round him through a mist. He had to make an effort in order to hear the words which the tuan besar was shouting at him. At last, out of the multitude of words hurled at him, one question penetrated his brain.

"Why did you run away?"

Why? wondered Ruki. Why had he run away? Behind his impassive face his thoughts struggled in an attempt to formulate an answer. He wanted to find an answer that would protect him from the dread white creature with the red face. It must avert the danger of that thundering voice.

"Why the hell did you run away? Will you answer me?"

Why? He had seen Karminah, and then he had seen nenneh, the buffalo, the campong. . . .

His downcast eyelids trembled before his eyes. He gave his reply very quietly, and he expressed himself in an image from his own language.

"Silap hati! My heart wandered away."

Then he cracked his fingers in all their joints, and waited resignedly for what was to come.

"Silap hati! Silap hati! Always the same nonsense. I'll teach you silap hati. Take him to the police, Ali."

"Yes, tuan besar."

The white figure disappeared. Ruki had been lucky: the manager had happened to feel disinclined to dirty his hands on a coolie. He had already more than enough bother over the case of Nur. What a fool that mandur had been to go and solve the riddle, and all over one of those confounded Chinese. As though China wasn't lousy with them! Millions starved to death every year in China, and now because a single one had been lynched by his coolies there was all this trouble with the government and with the courts.

Ruki waited, dazed with fear. Was nothing going to happen? Wasn't he going to be thrashed?

"Get up!" shouted the agent.

Ruki stood up. "Along with you, you son of a pig!"

Ali marched off, shouting insults at the top of his voice at Ruki, who marched in silence behind him. He no longer thought of running away.

As soon as they had turned a corner, Ali dropped his voice a little. Then he ceased to speak altogether.

"Have you any money?" asked Ali after a while.

"How should I have any money?" asked Ruki in return. "Why do you ask?"

They were perfectly amicable again.

"It's more pleasant to have a little money when one is in prison. Then one can buy cigarettes."

"I have no money," said Ruki. Then, half curious and half afraid, he asked: "What is it like in prison, agent?"

Ali shrugged his shoulders.

"Not very different from here," he said. "Here they order you about, and there they order you about. But there is one good thing about it: they feed you well. You even get a pickled egg once a week. But you are not allowed to have a light at night. You must sleep in the dark, and that's not pleasant. And you mustn't smoke at night either."

"Do they beat you in prison?"

"Sometimes," admitted Ali, and then, in a friendly tone he continued: "If they ask you to bear witness against Nur, you'd do well to do as they tell you. If you refuse, there is no saying but mandur Amat may beat you when you get back to the compound."

Ruki made no comment. He was still wondering what prison would be like. Nur used to say that it was quite agreeable, but even if it was unpleasant, what could he do about it? The tuan besar was sending him to prison, so there was nothing left for him to do but go there. And he would have to bear witness against Nur. He thought of all the humiliations to which Nur had submitted him. Allah was putting vengeance into his hands. This thought made him smile as he walked along. Certainly he would bear witness against Nur. He would do it on oath.

To the consequences of his evidence he gave no thought.

Ruki received eight days' imprisonment for desertion. He was also interrogated on the subject of the murder of the Chinese. His testimony provided the final proof of Nur's guilt. Nur got fifteen years' penal servitude in the coal mines of Sawah Lunto. This punishment was not merely for the murder of the Chinese: his former crime in Java was also taken into account. Which went to prove that the fate allotted to him by Allah had come to pass although he had run away from Java.

After Ruki had served his sentence, he was sent back to the estate, where he worked as before. He submitted to the yoke that white civilization had laid upon his shoulders.

# PART III

I

YEARS passed by, years made up of days that were all the same and that were filled with toil that never varied.

Ruki did not return to Java. Just as his first contract was on the point of running out, he was invited one evening by the head mandur to come to his room for a talk and a cup of coffee. The other coolies who had arrived with Ruki and would be free at about the same time were also invited. They were amazed to receive such an honour. They did not know that one of the head mandur's duties was to keep the coolies on the estate and to persuade them to sign new contracts.

Ruki borrowed a jacket and a turban from Iman and thus, dressed as custom dictated, went to the head mandur's hut. A small wooden building with two little rooms and a kitchen, it stood on the compound square of section one. As he entered diffidently, Ruki saw that the others were already sitting round the head mandur on the mat that covered the floor. They sat with their legs crossed, smoking in silence, and all of them were dressed in their best clothes or in clothes which, like Ruki, they had borrowed from a comrade in order to be dressed in sarong and turban according to custom.

Ruki greeted his host humbly. He was shy and

afraid. He had hitherto known the head mandur only at work, and there, as the tuan's representative, he had always been ready to use his fists. But now he was so friendly that he seemed like a father welcoming his son. Ruki joined the circle, and, with downcast eyes, muttered an unintelligible word of thanks when a large cup of black coffee was placed in front of him close to his crossed legs. He listened to the conversation without taking part in it. The talk fell mainly from the lips of the head mandur. He spoke of the work and of the estate. Two small oil lamps threw their reddish light on the quiet, attentive faces and on the squat figure of the head mandur who, instead of his usual khaki trousers and sun helmet, wore for the occasion a sarong and a meticulously folded turban of delicate batik.

He looks just like the chief of the campong, Ruki thought, eyeing him covertly as he bent carefully over the steaming coffee.

"And you, Ruki?" the head mandur said suddenly, turning towards him, "you are also on the point of being free. In three days' time your contract runs out."

"Yes, Pa," Ruki stammered, covered with confusion.

"Well, well, and what are you going to do? I suppose you intend to go back to Java?"

Ruki looked up in amazement. The head mandur had asked his intentions, the intentions of him who for three years had not been allowed to have an intention, a will of his own. He had forgotten that it was possible to make decisions, to intend, to have a will. The power of deciding had been beaten out of him, trodden underfoot and stifled. He had lost every idea of independence, and now abruptly he was asked: "What do you intend. . . ?" In three days' time he would be free, and he thought suddenly of nenneh and of how she would be too old to look after the buffalo any longer. He told his thoughts to the head mandur very gently, in a modest and subdued voice. He said that he wanted to go back to Java in order to work his rice-field. He was tired of the hard and heavy tasks on the estate. He was tired of the ton-tong and of the lack of freedom. He longed for his campong. He told how in his dreams he heard the murmur of his river and the mumblings of the old men at their prayers. Yes, he would like to go back.

The head mandur listened with a benevolent smile, nodding in agreement from time to time. Of course, of course. Ruki was right. The contract work was heavy, it made one ache right into one's bones, didn't it? And one's heart had a way of wandering back to the place of one's birth, for there the body rested more softly when the hour of death arrived. How well the head mandur seemed to understand everything! There was no trace in him of the severe and merciless task-master. He was more like a patient, understanding priest to whom one could tell one's sins. He was a father, an old friend. His voice flowed through the little room like a peaceful river and carried with it the attention of his audience, carried it in the direction which he chose to take.

"But, Ruki, what about the campong, and the people in the campong? What will they say when you return to them? Won't they all ask: 'Ruki, where have you come from? Where have you been all this time?' And won't they also ask: 'What have you brought back with you, you who have been to the country where gold is cheap. . . ?'

"And then what will you reply, my son? You will have to say, won't you: 'Oh, but I was only a coolie.' You will have to say: 'I did not even become a mandur. I toiled in the stinking water of the swamps. I wore myself out in the damp gloom of the virgin forest. My back ached as I dug the naked, scorched land. And I have been to prison.' You will say: 'But I am back now, though I am poorer than when I went away.' You will have to tell them that you have returned half naked because you do not possess even a jacket. When they hold slamatan in the campong, you will not even be able to dress according to custom, for you have only your little pair of shorts. 'I have not even brought a wife with me,' you will have to admit, 'for I had no woman there. I had only those whom I could seduce into infidelity and take away from their own men, bad women . . .'

"Will not the men of the campong mock you then, my son? And will they not point at you and call out: 'Look, here is Ruki who has come back naked from the country where gold is cheap,' and will not your nenneh bow her face to the ground in shame because her grandson was so foolish? And you? Will you not, instead of the murmur of your river and the mumblings of the prayers of the old men, hear the jeering of those who were your friends?"

Ruki's head drooped. He sat quite still in front of his empty coffee cup. His cigarette had gone out in his hand. Opposite him was the expectant, silent figure of the head mandur, who had spoken to him simply and directly as a father.

"Yes, Pa."

The others too had bowed their heads. What applied to Ruki applied to every one of them.

"Why not sign once more?" asked the head mandur. "The second contract is only for eighteen months. That won't be long. You are no longer a new coolie. You will no longer be beaten, for you know the work and all the rules. Who knows, perhaps you will get a woman. Perhaps you will become mandur. Then you will be able to put money on one side. Then you can go home wealthy. You can buy a buffalo and another rice-field. You will take gold with you when you go back. Why not sign again?"

"Yes, Pa."

"And if you sign again you will get another advance. Twenty guilders."

The coolies looked up, surprised. Twenty guilders! That was much money.

"I'll sign again, Pa, and I'll go back in eighteen months."

Ruki signed again, and so did the others. The head mandur got a premium for each of them, but in those days Ruki did not know that.

Eighteen months did not seem a long time. He

received his twenty guilders and he gambled for two nights. Then all the money had gone. He had not bought a jacket, neither had he bought a turban. And his couch was still bare, without a mat, without a pillow. Everything was as it had been.

The eighteen months passed, and Ruki signed again. He did not need to be told this time that one could not go back to Java poor. Once more he received twenty guilders, but he was wiser this time and did not gamble it away. He went to the Malay campong to buy a jacket and a turban, for this time when his contract was finished, he meant to go back. But in a Chinese shop he saw a clock. It was a clock that played a tune four times an hour. He forgot what he had intended to buy and bought the clock. It cost twenty guilders. Perfectly happy, he carried it back to the compound. He could not read the time it told, for he had never learned to do so. But he listened to the little tune and to the regular ticking, and he found it a delight to wind up the clock with the key. It gave him as much pleasure as a new toy gives a child, and he did not think of the fact that he had bought it with eighteen months of the life of his body and his soul. His companions also thought the clock marvellous. For two months it ticked in their bachelors' hut and played tunes. Then it stopped. Ruki had dropped it one day by accident. The glass was broken too, and henceforth it hung on the dusty wall without voice, without heart, mute and dead. Nobody looked at it any more. The inside grew rusty from the moist air of the night that entered through the crevices of the wooden walls. One day Ruki sold it to a Chinese for a guilder. He gambled away the guilder—it happened to be hari besar.

Thus did Ruki's life pass. Time grew. The rubber trees grew. Their shadow covered the bare, carefully weeded ground where the mimosa flourished no longer. A factory had been constructed where the rubber was made into brown sheets. It brought two new things into the pure, quiet, even days: the stench of rubber and the drone of machinery. The regular beat of the machines came to be the pulse of the newly reclaimed land. If it ceased for one moment, the coolies looked up and asked one another: "What has happened? The factory is not working."

New coolies no longer arrived in large numbers. Only now and then one came to fill a place that had been left vacant. For the work had ceased to expand. It grew monotonous, ending where it began, and beginning where it ended. Every day brought the same task for the coolies: tapping, weeding, tapping, weeding, and they had become accustomed to the iron rules and to the sound of the ton-tong. They had grown old at their tasks; they were like tamed animals that have lost the capacity to live in freedom.

One thing only marked a change in the monotonous order of things: the arrival and departure of the tuans. They came from other estates and went to other estates. When they grew fat and pot-bellied, they either became tuan besar or returned to Holland. But they no longer scolded with the same verve, and they were not so ready with their fists.

It made contract work easier. The cage had grown almost comfortable, and no one sought its door.

In the course of all these years, Java had faded into a vague and ever more distant shadow. Nenneh must be dead by now, said Ruki to himself sometimes, and the buffalo has surely been killed.

Years ago Ruki had become a tapper. Every day he cut the same trees, the very trees he had helped to plant. Every day he collected the latex and carried it to the reception shed. His hand now knew no other work. He stepped lightly down the rows of trees, past the sticks on which hung the white porcelain cups. Every day he made the same round, and he did not dislike the work. He knew it so thoroughly that he was incapable of making mistakes, and therefore he was never reprimanded. It is true that he did not understand the reason of his work. He had no idea what happened to the brown sheets of rubber once they had been packed in boxes and sent away by train. He accepted without reflection. He no longer wondered at the impressive regularity of the machines. It had become a matter of course to him that a factory stood there whose metallic drone drowned the echoes of the tropical forest. Before his eyes was taking place the evolution from primitive nature to modern technique. He had been rudely shaken from his pre-historic dream and had awakened in the white civilization of the twentieth century. All the centuries in between had been jumped. He knew nothing of the Titanic struggle of the human brain with the forces of nature, and for this reason he felt no amazement and no emotion at the sight of the factory walls and the factory chimneys where recently mighty trees had grown.

It was all the doing of the blandas, and he accepted it without question. Just as there was a sun and a moon, there was also a factory with its boxes and its rubber, a train, the telephone posts, and motor cars. Sometimes he stepped into one of these motor cars—they were old Ford vans re-built by the Chinese—and then he went to the little town nearby. It cost him fivepence. There was a bazaar there. And a cinematograph which he had visited once. He had thought it splendid. The whole evening he had sat, in amazed silence, his mouth wide open.

Still he had no woman. Nor had he any friends. Kromorejo was in section one. They hardly ever met. Karminah had gone away, so he had been told. He did not know whither. Life was rather lonely, without family, without wife or child. But Ruki was getting a little older each day. He had grown used to loneliness. His body had become stronger, work had made it tough. He had grown a moustache, and for this reason some of the younger coolies called him "Pa."

Apart from a sleeping mat, he had no possessions, for he continued to be in debt to the free women. The few coins that remained to him from his wages he gambled away. Such was life, thought Ruki. It was his fate. His nassip. . . .

II

IN the still dark evening the soft rain was like a hesitating murmur that ran through the other and harsher sounds from the compound.

Ruki was sharpening his tapping knife in front of his hut, doubled up towards the circle of light thrown by his little lamp. Outside the circle of light the porch was dark, but he knew that on an empty box lying on its side sat Sentono, smoking in silence. From time to time a little fiery point became more marked in the vague darkness. It was Sentono's cigarette, at which he was drawing now and then.

"Aren't you going to sharpen your knife, Sentono?"

"No more knife sharpening for me, mate. My contract is over. I want to go home. I have been here over twenty years, and I am old. I am going back to Java."

"What do you want in Java, Sentono? It is better perhaps to stay here. You have your little room, your rice. Perhaps it is more difficult to find food in Java."

Sentono continued to smoke. His slow thoughts hung vaguely amidst the sound of the irregularly dripping rain. The cigarette remained in his hand, its lighted point turned towards his palm. It made his hand into a small cup throwing out a faint glimmer that slowly, very slowly faded and went out.

"I cannot help thinking continually of my dessa," said Sentono, and his voice sounded dreamy as though it were carried on the wings of memory. He threw away the end of the cigarette.

"I think continually of my parents, of my brothers and my sister. I left a rice-field behind, and a house. It is always in my memory. I see it in my dreams. I can no longer work. My hand is uncertain when I tap the trees. Sometimes I forget a few. My heart has wandered away. I must go home."

With his thumb Ruki felt carefully along the edge of his knife. Then he lit a cigarette from the flame of the oil lamp. He leaned against the wall.

"And will you return here?"

"Perhaps," Sentono declared, continuing to meditate aloud. "You never know how things turn out. If it is my fate to return here, I shall return."

Ruki was silent. He too was thinking of Java. He imagined Sentono in Java, and he saw him on a grassy plain under the sunny sky near the foot of a volcano. He saw him coming down a narrow winding path and crossing the open square of the campong. Then he saw him entering nenneh's house. He could not picture Sentono's return in any other way. He thought of the river, of bathing there.

"And your woman?" he asked suddenly. "Wirio? Her contract is not over yet. We arrived together, and I have still six months to serve."

"So has she. She is staying here."

A long silence followed. Then Ruki asked: "Can I have your woman for the time being? If you come back, I will return her to you, and if you don't come back I will keep her."

"All right," said Sentono, "if the tuan will give her to you."

He did not care who took his woman. His heart was no longer there. His thoughts dwelt only in his memories. He was not sharpening his knife, for tomorrow another man would perform his task. Tomorrow he would put on his new kaïn and his new turban. Wirio had saved two hundred guilders and three gold coins for him. He was taking them with him, together with his sleeping mat and his pillow. The other things—some kitchen utensils, a hen with seven chicks, his little lamp, his woman—these he left behind. It was the end of his existence as a contract coolie. He did not care who had the woman after him.

Next day Ruki squatted before the house of the assistant.

"What do you want, Ruki?"

Ruki cleared his throat and began in a leisurely way: "Tabeh, tuan. I ask tuan's pardon, but I have been under contract for many years, and still I have no woman. I am growing old, but still I have no woman. There is nobody to cook for me, nobody who washes for me. I greet tuan, and I crave pardon, but Sentono is returning to Java now and his woman Wirio is staying behind. Now I ask tuan if it is agreeable to tuan that I should be given Sentono's woman."

Meekly he waited for a reply.

"Have you talked about it with the head mandur?"

"I have talked about it with my mandur, and my mandur has talked about it with the head mandur, and the head mandur said it is right if the tuan is agreeable."

"If that is so, you have my approval, Ruki. You have been here for a long time, and you are entitled to it. You can move into Sentono's hut."

"Yes, tuan. I beg your pardon, tuan. Tabeh, tuan."

"Tabeh."

Stooping as long as he was in front of the house, Ruki crept away. Only when he reached the road did he draw himself up. This was in accordance with the rules of good manners.

He went straight to his hut, rolled up his sleeping mat, and put it on Sentono's couch. Wirio was cooking while he made his arrangements. She looked up.

"Are you living here in this hut now?"

"Yes," said Ruki. "Tuan has said I may live here."

Thus the matter was settled.

Wirio gave him his evening meal, just as she had given Sentono his the evening before. He ate his food sitting on the couch, his legs crossed. The little lamp stood by his side. Wirio's shadow moved along the wall as she tidied away the pans and the plates on a board covering the hen and her chicks, which were huddled together in an old basket. Then she began to comb her hair. She took off her jacket and knotted her sarong under her arms.

Ruki belched from satisfaction. He had never before eaten enough since he had come to the estate. His eyes wandered round the hut. It was his now. The cooking utensils, the three white plates, and the blue enamelled mug were his. So were the hen and the woman. She had stretched out on the couch by his side against the wall. She had no looks left, she was old. Her son Païdi was a man, a contract coolie himself. Her breasts were loose and withered, her neck was dry and scraggy. She had little hair left, and one of her front teeth was missing. She was ugly and inspired no desire. But in Ruki desire had died long since. His blood was quiet. His body wanted only two things: rest and food.

He was growing old. It was not without reason that more and more people were coming to call him "Pa Ruki."

III

IT was hari besar. Wirio and Ruki went out to do their shopping. The motor coach took them to the centre of the little town, and they walked together to the market.

Ruki walked in front, and Wirio followed. This was as it should be in their world. Ruki wore a new jacket and a turban. He had just renewed his contract, and with the money he had received Wirio had bought clothes for him. She had changed the balance for two small gold coins that were now adorning her vest. She seemed very small and shrunken as she walked there in her tight black jacket and her smooth sarong, with a thin silken green slendang round her lean shoulders, following humbly the man to whom she belonged. But for all her meekness, it was Wirio who managed Ruki's existence.

"We must buy some nangka," he said, "I haven't eaten nangka since I came to Deli."

"Good. But we will buy nangka not only for you but also to sell to-night in the compound. Then we shall make a little profit."

Ruki followed his own train of thought.

"On the edge of my campong stood a tall nangka tree," he said to her. "Nobody planted it there. It just shot up from a heap of refuse, all by itself."

Wirio made no reply. She was reckoning how much profit she could make on a twenty-pound jack fruit if she bought the whole. Much did she care whether a jack fruit tree had grown in Ruki's campong. She did not even know its name. She came from an entirely different territory in central Java, and of her birthplace Ruki knew nothing. That was why she never talked of her former life. What was the good of it? She had left a husband there. Probably he had died long ago. And if he hadn't died, he was sure to have taken another wife, and in any case he had long since forgotten her and Païdi. And Païdi had grown up and knew nothing of his own father.

"Now is the time for nangka," Ruki said. "Look, they are selling it everywhere."

He pointed to a little stall by the side of the road. It stood at the entrance to a small garden where all kinds of flowers and sweet potatoes and maize were growing. Through this wealth of growing things a narrow path led to a small but tidy wooden house. Before the veranda door hung white curtains, and on the walls prints in old discoloured gilded frames. There was also a hat-stand, and a man's dirty grey felt hat was suspended from one of the pegs.

"Don't let's buy here," said Wirio. "It will be dearer. I want to buy a whole fruit in the market. Then we can open it at home and it will come out much cheaper."

But Ruki was obstinate. "You can buy a whole fruit in the market, but I want a few pieces now. This one is such a lovely yellow that my heart aches with pain, I long so much to know its taste again."

As he spoke he stopped in front of the stall. A woman was sitting behind it making small parcels of banana leaf in which she wrapped big chunks of yellow jack fruit. From time to time she chased away the flies with a palm leaf fan. She wore several heavy gold rings on her fingers, and there was gold on her jacket.

"Do you want to buy nangka?" she asked without interrupting her work.

"Yes," replied Ruki. "What is the price of a parcel?"

"A penny."

Wirio secretly nudged him. That meant that she thought it too expensive. But Ruki took no notice. He helped himself to two parcels and from his tobacco box he fished out among the brass coins a silver twopenny piece.

"Where do you come from?" asked the woman as she handed the fruit to Ruki.

"We come from far away," said Ruki. "We come from Bukit Radjah, and we are going to the market. But I had such a longing to eat nangka at once. I haven't tasted it for many years."

"Bukit Radjah?" repeated the woman with a puzzled expression on her face. "I used to be there too. But it's so very long ago. I was housekeeper there."

Ruki looked at her face with more attention than before. She was old and fat, but there was still something handsome about her face. He felt vaguely that he had seen her before. But where, he wondered.

"Housekeeper? At Bukit Radjah?"

"Yes, to tuan Dunk. First I was a coolie, but not for long. Then the tuan sent for me from the compound."

Wirio suddenly looked up, and with her sharp little eyes searched the woman's face.

"Eh! Karminah!" She put the corner of her slendang before her mouth and chuckled.

Karminah looked up with surprise. "Yes, indeed, I am Karminah."

"Karminah!" repeated Ruki in amazement. "Well, well, Karminah! I did not recognize you. I am Ruki."

Now it was her turn to clap her hands in amazement.

"Ruki! Ts . . . ts . . . ts. . . . On the same ship did we come from Java. Ts . . . ts . . . ts . . . ! And now I didn't recognize you. You have grown a moustache."

Karminah laughed. Her laugh was a little too loud. That was because she had been a housekeeper for so many years. And she still wore a white jacket trimmed with lace. She hardly looked at Wirio and conversed only with Ruki.

"And I've grown fat," she said, "but you must know I've had two children. Girls, both of them."

"Children!" repeated Ruki.

"Yes, but they are in Holland. The tuan took them with him."

"Tuan Dunk?"

"Yes. At first he did not want me to have children 'If you become pregnant,' he used to say, 'I'll send you back to the compound and you can dig the ground again.' That's why he sent away his former housekeeper, because she was with child." Karminah smiled. Absent-mindedly she shifted a few parcels of fruit. "But what are you to do if Allah sends you a child? Tuan was very angry. But when it was born it was a girl. It had a lovely, pale yellow skin and had the same face as tuan. Then he was no longer quite so angry. He was very kind to me. Two years later, after tuan had been transferred to Tanah Bukit, the second one was born. It was also a girl. And when tuan returned to the white country they had grown tall. I think the elder was eight. He wanted to take them with him. That's much better for them. There are many schools where they can learn. . . . Perhaps that will make them clever, and perhaps they will marry blandas."

She was silent and played with the palm leaf fan. A distant thought passed behind her smooth face. Then she smiled and said quietly: "Anyhow, if they had stayed with me they would only have grown into campong children. Won't you sit down a moment and smoke a cigarette?"

She pointed to the small wooden bench that stood by the side of the stall. Ruki sat down, drew one leg up under him, and lit a cigarette. Wirio remained standing. She held herself a little apart, rather shy and a trifle reluctant.

"So you gave your children to the tuan?"

Karminah nodded. "He made me sign a paper.

He promised to give me a little house if I did. So perhaps it was all for the best." Across her shoulder she pointed with her thumb. "That's the house he gave me. The tuan's hat-stand is still there in the veranda, and that is one of the tuan's hats. I was housekeeper to another tuan for a few years, but he was always drunk. Tuan Dunk was a good tuan. I still have a portrait of him, and the two children are on it too. But now they are much bigger, and perhaps they no longer look like the portrait. I am sure they are quite different from the memory I have kept of them."

"And do you live here all by yourself now, Karminah?"

"Oh dear, just fancy doing that!" Karminah laughed again. "I am married now," she continued. "My husband is a tailor. He makes jackets and trousers and sometimes also clothes for children. Is this your woman?"

These were the first words she had addressed, even indirectly, to Wirio.

"Yes," said Ruki, "she is my woman Wirio. Surely you remember her. She too came on the same boat."

Karminah again clapped her hands together. "Yes, Wirio. But surely she had a child?"

"He is grown up," said Wirio with quiet dignity. "He is a coolie now. He is a tapper."

Karminah shook her head. Was it really so long ago that the three of them had come from Java?

"Are you going back to Java, Ruki?"

"Perhaps I shall go back one day. When I have a little money I shall go back. And you, Karminah?"

"I?" she said. She cracked the joints of her fingers very slowly one at a time. Then, with half a smile and half a shrug of the shoulders, she said: "I shall stay. That's the best thing for me. My children are in the white country, my husband is here. I have a house. All my life is here, that is very clear. And what should I go to seek in Java? My parents are surely dead by now, and I am no longer young. Allah has ordained it as it is."

Ruki nodded.

"I still often think of that shed in Java. Do you remember it, Karminah?"

"When I cried so much," she said, "and when you gave me cake to eat, and later on the boat when the sailor wanted to beat me."

"And when we had so far to walk, right down to the estate. Your foot was bleeding, for you had hurt it on a stone. And then afterwards on the estate you were given to Marto."

"Yes," she said with a smile, "and the head mandur beat you."

Ruki threw away his cigarette, gathered his sarong together, and fastened it with a fresh knot.

"It's all so long ago. Now we have grown old. If I come to the market ag ain, I shall come to see you, Karminah, for we arrived on the same boat, did we not?"

"We still remain shipmates. Good luck attend you!" Karminah started to make up little parcels of fruit again, fixing each one with a piece of fibre. Her face showed no emotion. But when Ruki rose to take his leave, she handed him a parcel of fruit.

"Take this with you," she said, "because once you gave me cake when I cried."

"Thank you. Good luck to you, Karminah!"

Ruki once more led the way. Behind him walked Wirio. She scarcely acknowledged Karminah's parting good wishes: throughout the conversation she had felt a stranger and an outsider. To think that Karminah still wore a housekeeper's jacket trimmed with lace although she had become a respectably married woman!

"Karminah has really grown fat," said Ruki. "When we came from Java, you remember, she was as slender as a child."

"Fat!" replied Wirio. "All housekeepers grow fat. That comes from being lazy and eating pig's meat." Contemptuously she spat out a wide jet of betel juice, but she did it behind Ruki's back. He did not see her do it. He was eating his jack fruit, and reflecting that it was almost as sweet as that he had eaten long ago in the campong.

IV

SENTONO did not come back. So Wirio stayed with Ruki. But she did not sign another contract. She became a free woman. He learned much from her. He learned how to deal with mandurs, and how to get an easy job. He became compound sweeper. The whole day long he had nothing to do but sweep the large square. He sent up clouds of dust which whirled about him and disappeared into the air. He gathered the dirt and the refuse and burned it in stoves made for the purpose. Why this had to be done was a thing he failed to understand. He did it because he had been ordered to do so. He made toys for the children. He hammered together a little stall for Wirio, and on pay nights and when it was hari besar she sold sweetmeats and syrup. He gave up gambling—Wirio cured him of his passion for it. She was industrious and economical. She cooked not only for Ruki, but for the new coolies and for the bachelors. They gave their money to her now in the same way as Ruki had formerly given his money to other free women. She looked after the chickens and sold the young hens and cockerels to the Chinese shopkeeper. As she had once slaved and saved for Sentono, now she devoted herself to Ruki, and thus did Ruki grow rich.

It is true that he was also growing old. He no longer knew how old he was. Maybe he was almost fifty, he thought. The tuans called him Pa Ruki now, and they treated him with the friendliness one shows to an older person.

At night, when it was moonlight, the young men and the new coolies sat in a circle round him and listened to his stories of the old days when there were no motor cars and no labour inspectors to whom one could complain when one had been beaten.

He told them of the work of reclamation, of the cutting of the forest, of the Chinese who used to work on the estate. He told them how they used to entice the women away from the compound because they had no women of their own in their camp. He told them how he had once run away because he kept thinking of Java and how he had borne witness against Nur who had killed the Chinese, for it was all so long ago that Ruki believed that Nur had really done the deed, and that it was for that crime he had been punished with fifteen years' penal servitude.

Of Saïma he said not a word. He still remembered how she had died while the native midwife massaged her body in order to get the child out of it. She had not screamed while it happened because Mohammedan women do not scream in childbirth. It would be a shameful thing to do. But one could hear her stifled groans when one passed by her hut. She was dead by the time the doctor arrived, and the child had been born already. It was dead. It was a boy. Its skin was very pale yellow, said the midwife, and it had slanting Chinese eyes. It had been buried with Saima in the coolie graveyard behind the hospital. But a man does not talk about such things. They are women's gossip, and that is why he only told the story of mandur Amat who was so dreadfully severe but who had long since returned to Java. He told them of the tuan besar who never did anything but curse and scold, and of the assistant who thrashed a man for every little mistake.

Now everything had changed for the better.

"The work is finished," said Ruki, and what he meant was that for the blandas the work had been all that mattered, and that it was the work that had been to blame.

The novices who sat around him also told stories. It appeared from what they said that in Java, too, life was not what it used to be. When he heard these stories, Ruki's eyes stared ahead of him. His eyes were no longer as dark as they had been. Round the pupil was a grey circle, the first shadow of approaching old age. But these changed eyes saw an unchanged image that had never faded: the grassy plain, the volcano, the campong, nenneh. No, the image had not faded. Sometimes it had moved into the background, but now it shone all the more vividly in his memory. He no longer realized that nenneh must of course be dead, and that the buffalo could not possibly be alive. He forgot that thirty years had elapsed, that the campong had perhaps been moved, and that there might be no trace left of the little deserted graveyard. He forgot that his childhood companions had grown as old as he had, and that from them a new generation had issued. He saw all things as he had left them behind more clearly than he had ever seen them in reality. For he did not see with his eyes now, but with his soul which detached itself from his body and roamed away in the night, to bring back on its tranquil outstretched hands sweet pictures of his childhood.

In his dreams the grassland flourished. Behind it sprang up the volcano, standing out blue against the blue sky. He could see the anthills, the tai-ajam bushes, the old derelict graveyard, and the buffaloes which lifted their heads and bellowed as evening fell. There was the sinuous path dropping into the depths where the river roared over the boulders. In the white moonlight, the ramshackle houses stood dreamily on their curved stakes. The bamboo with its waving branches was outlined against the white sky, and the broad shields of the banana leaves trembled as the moonbeams broke on them. And nenneh slept by his side, mumbling with her betel reddened mouth, her chest sunken like that of an old bird.

Once more the almost petrified desire for Java came to life within Ruki's breast. Like a waterspout drawn up by a sudden whirlwind, it sprang up in his heart. It was a deep blue dream of an ideal that grew up from his flat existence, and rose into a lofty cone of longing and desire. It was homesickness.

Homesickness had him in its grip. His last contract had run out.

"I want to go home, tuan. I have grown old. I

have been here for nearly thirty years, and now I do not want to sign again. I have money, tuan, and I think of my campong. My woman Wirio will accompany me."

The assistant looked at Ruki's expressionless face. He saw an old coolie, weather-beaten and worn by toil.

"That's right, Ruki. Call here the day after to-morrow when hari besar is over, and I will give you a note to the office."

"Yes, tuan. Thank you, tuan."

Ruki crept away. "The day after to-morrow," he said to Wirio, "then we are leaving."

Wirio continued to stir the contents of her broad, black pan. "The day after to-morrow," was all she said. But when she had finished cooking she began to clean and polish everything. She caught the hens and tied them together by their feet.

"What are you doing?" asked Ruki.

"I am going to sell everything," she replied. "We cannot take the chickens and the pans with us."

An hour later she came back. She brought twelve guilders with her. From behind a loose board in the wall she took a little tin. She opened it. It was full of money. Ruki sat by her side on the couch. They put the money together and sorted it. Then they counted it.

"Two hundred and thirty-five guilders," said Ruki. His fingers felt over the little piles of silver coins and over Wirio's golden sovereigns. With trembling hands he smoothed the bank-notes. "We are rich, Wirio. We can buy a buffalo and a house."

"And a rice-field," said Wirio.

Ruki made no reply. He thought of the water that was led down from the mountain in babbling streams through the rice-fields. He thought of the ripening paddy.

It was the evening of pay-day. The gamelan sent its deep, humming, metallic sound over the thronged square. Many voices and footsteps passed by their hut. But they did not listen. They were both sitting on the couch looking at the money that lay between them. Then Wirio put out her hand.

"What do you want?" asked Ruki.

"To put it away," she said, and she returned the coins to the tin, folded the paper money over them, and returned it all behind the loose board.

"Come along. Go to sleep," she said.

She undid her bun. Most of her hair was false. It was her own hair that she had kept carefully and knotted into a long tress. Now she suspended it from a nail in the wall and combed her hair. It was a long time before she was ready. Ruki did not look at her. He thought of the day after to-morrow.

"Let's sleep," repeated Wirio. She crept behind him and stretched herself out with a yawn. Ruki also lay down. His hands were under his head, his eyes stared into the dusk. A tiny circle of light trembled round the oil lamp. A house lizard crept around it, and with a lightning dart of its tongue caught a mosquito. Somewhere in a corner of the hut a rat was gnawing a hole. Ruki listened to it. He listened to the other sounds that came from outside. There was laughter, revelry, animated conversation. And the sound of the gamelan. A man somewhere was saying his prayer aloud in a monotonous, sing-song voice.

Wirio had fallen asleep. She snored with wide-open mouth.

He could not sleep. It was the night of pay-day. The free women were standing behind their stalls selling sweetmeats. Many people sauntered past, chattering and laughing. Some of them wore their best clothes.

He would go among them once more, thought Ruki. For so many years he had done nothing but work. He had worked in the rubber garden and in the compound square, and during his free hours he had worked for Wirio. He had cut wood, carried water, rasped the coconut, and made utensils from coconut shells and tins. Just this once he wanted to be free. The day after to-morrow he was going away. This was his last pay-day.

Very softly he rose. He put on his new jacket and his new kaïn. He folded his new turban on his head. He did it very slowly, as though preparing for a ceremony. Then he felt in the pocket of his old coat and found several small silver coins. He wanted to buy some sweetmeats.

He crossed the compound square, making his way through the crowd that was surging there.

Was this the same place he had seen so often on similar nights? It seemed different to him, strange, novel. He loitered past the mats on which the Malays were displaying their wares, past the smoking red wicks of the oil lamps and the stalls of the free women. He bought fruit and cake and syrup, and the syrup made him think of the man from Batavia who had lured him away from his campong. What would Sidin and Karimun say now if he showed them his money? If they could see him go to the market and come home with a new buffalo? And nenneh. . . ? As he moved on slowly, he dreamed the dream that absorbed all his thoughts.

He halted near the entrance to the gambling shed. He heard the little tops spinning on the plates.

"Wah! . . . klabang!"

There was laughter. Again a top span. There was a deep silence of expectation. Ruki looked on. How often he had sat there himself in former days. But since Wirio's time all that had changed. He smiled as he saw them gambling, putting in their stakes, winning, losing. There was the same little mat with its crude drawings in black and red paint on each of the squares. He could not drag his eyes away from the mat.

The frog. . . . Ruki bent forward and threw a cent on to the frog. The top was put in motion, spun and spun and dropped on its side with a rattle. The lid was removed. It was the serpent. Again Ruki bent forward. He placed a cent on the meeting point of four square. He listened tensely to the spinning of the top, and he told himself vaguely that he had still nine cents in his pocket, and wanted to gamble with them. He wanted to gamble again. The day after to-morrow he was to go. If he lost his cents, he would go to bed.

He lost them. He was standing dreamily and

looking on when somebody said: "Aren't you playing any more, Pa Ruki?"

He did not answer at once.

"I'm going back to Java the day after to-morrow," he said at last. Nobody listened to him. The top had finished spinning. Once more it showed the frog.

Ruki walked back slowly to his hut. He stood in front of the couch. Wirio was asleep and did not hear him come in. The lamp was smoking. He turned it down a little. He did so without noticing what he did. On other nights he had not noticed when it smoked: there was a broad black mark of smoke on the brown boarding. Then he bent towards the place where he knew that Wirio kept the money hidden. From the tin he took a guilder and a few twopenny pieces. With this money he returned to the shed. First he staked the small coins, then the guilder. He lost everything. Once more he returned to his hut. Hesitating, he stood with the tin in his hand. He became dimly conscious of the thought that it would be better to go to sleep. But he could not sleep: there were so many voices. There was the sound of the gamelan. He took two rix-dollars and a guilder's worth of small change. This time he was hardly aware of the amount he took. Hastily he returned the tin to its place. He had decided to gamble on another mat, and no longer to stake on the frog. The frog had not brought him any luck. He would follow the centipede and win back what he had lost.

Quietly he slipped back among the gamblers.

They were bending over the covered plate, listening while the top unravelled their fate.

With scarcely a movement Ruki gambled as in a dream. He was sitting very straight, his face a mask without movement. He heard neither the exclamations of the others nor their laughter nor their silence. He was aware of the little top only, of the black and red drawings of the animals, of the coins that were lying on them. All he knew was that he was losing.

Round the mat a circle of spectators had formed. A strong bond linked them together. They watched in silence. They noticed that Ruki kept raising his stakes, and continued to lose. The centipede was not bringing him luck either.

When he had lost his last stake he stared ahead of him for a moment. Then he rose. He returned to his hut, took the whole tin, and came back with it. Once more he settled down by the mat. The others looked with amazement at all this money. He played like one possessed and out of his senses. Without seeing what he did, he put down the coins one by one as his fingers happened to touch them. He played without the slightest trace of emotion, cool, self-possessed, seemingly indifferent, with slow movements and downcast eyes. But all the rigidity of his movements betrayed more and more the automatism, the fatalistic character of his actions.

He gambled away everything—the money, the gold coins, his clothes. At last with naked torso and wearing only his shorts, he returned to his hut. He walked quietly. A little bowed, perhaps, as he had come to walk of late. He was a gaunt, worn-out old coolie, a quiet phantom in the darkness through which was just beginning to glimmer the very first signs of dawn. As he entered, Wirio started up out of her sleep. She sat up at once, frightened by the figure at the side of the couch.

"Lah-illah-Allah, how you frightened me! I thought it was a thief!"

"It's me," said Ruki. He took his tobacco box and rolled himself a cigarette.

"Where have you come from? And why are you all undressed?"

Ruki made no reply. She looked at him inquisitively. Suddenly her suspicions were roused. She jumped up, bent towards the loose board, and groped with her fingers for the tin.

"Where is the money?" she shouted in a sudden knowledge of where he had been and what he had done. She was shouting close to his face. "You've been gambling, haven't you? You've been gambling, and you've lost, Have you lost everything?"

"I have lost," said Ruki. He sat down on the couch, his legs crossed beneath him.

"Allah! Allah!" she moaned. "Allah! Allah!" She seized her hair in both hands and swayed her body to and fro. "Allah! Allah! Allah! Allah!"

"Don't shout like that," said Ruki. "The mandur will hear you, and then he'll be angry."

Groaning, she searched again behind the board. When once more she found only the empty space where hitherto she had always found the tin, she became furious. She shook her fists at him.

"You men!" she shrieked, "you are beasts, all of you! You are good for nothing, nothing but eating and gambling, and you cannot even win. Gambling and losing! All the things for which I worked, all the things I put on one side, all I had saved up! What must we live on now in Java?"

Ruki made no reply. His face did not even show that he had heard her words. Was he asking himself the same question?

He sat with downcast head, and smoked. His eyelids were closed, his face was smooth. Between them there hung a deep silence. It was a silence that nothing could affect, nothing could remove. Wirio noticed it. She too became silent. She blew out the lamp and began to comb her hair very quietly. Her fingers were slow at the work. Then she looked at Ruki.

"Lie down and go to sleep," she said. "You have not slept the whole night."

He acted as though he had not heard her; but when she had left the hut and had drawn the door to behind her, he stretched himself out on the couch. He threw away his cigarette end, and, slipping his hand under his cheek, he fell asleep.

The day had hardly dawned when Ruki squatted down before the assistant's house. He was shivering. The wind was damp, and he wore only his shorts. When he heard a sound in the house he coughed.

"Is that you, Pa Ruki?"

"Yes, tuan."

"Oh yes, you've come to get your dismissal note."

"I beg your pardon, tuan, I should like to sign again."

The assistant looked down in amazement upon the crouching figure.

"Why have you come all undressed like this, Ruki, and without a jacket? Have you forgotten your manners?"

Ruki bent his face down to the ground. "I have no jacket, tuan."

"No jacket? Surely you had several? Where are they?"

"I have no longer got them, tuan."

"Surely you haven't been gambling?"

"Yes, tuan. I have been gambling."

"And you have lost?"

"I have lost, tuan."

"But your money?"

"I have lost it, tuan. I have nothing left, and now I should like to sign a contract. My woman must buy pots and pans, for she has nothing with which to cook."

There was a silence. Ruki imagined that the tuan must be very angry. But the tuan was not angry. He only shook his head. When he spoke again there was a strange, unwonted sound in his voice.

"So you will have to work again, Ruki. Do you think that in this way you will ever go back to your campong?"

Ruki continued to stare at the ground.

"And if you die here one day, Ruki, and have to be buried here in this strange earth? What then, Ruki?"

For a moment Ruki seemed to hesitate about his reply. Then he looked up. He looked past the assistant at something which perhaps only he could see. Behind those old resigned eyes, in which all desire had been extinguished, a quiet light seemed to burn, and with a very slight gesture of the shoulders he said, very softly: "Nassip. If it is the fate of a man . . . If Allah has ordained it thus . . . ?"

Once more he signed the contract. He did it without disappointment, without remorse, without bitterness.

He signed again for a year and a half.

It was the nineteenth time.